HOT FOR TEACHER

SHAKESPEARE MADE US FALL IN LOVE

FELICIA CARPARELLI

5 PRINCE PUBLISHING

Published by 5 PRINCE PUBLISHING & BOOKS, LLC

PO Box 865, Arvada, CO 80001

www.5PrinceBooks.com

ISBN digital: 978-1-63112-290-3

ISBN print: 978-1-63112-291-0

Cover Credit: Marianne Nowicki

To Jen and Pete, Tina, Davy and Eleanor;
for your support and love.

ACKNOWLEDGMENTS

Thank you, Bernadette for welcoming me into the 5 Prince family and thank you, Cate for your amazing edits and suggestions.

To all the Gotham Writer's teachers and colleagues I worked with on improving my craft, I thank you.

HOT FOR TEACHER

CHAPTER ONE

"To be or not to be, that is the question," quoted a tall, skinny man in Juliet West's adult Intro to Literature class. "But what is it really? What does Hamlet mean? What is the question?" He was so serious and so young; his bowtie quivered as he spoke. His voice cracked a little on the syllable *ques* before it dropped dramatically on the *tion.*

A deep voice guffawed in the back of the classroom. "Yeah, what is the question, teacher?"

Juliet sighed and put down her glasses. She knew that deep voice, she knew it well, after only thirty minutes. It belonged to the blond, muscular hunk in the back of the class. The older guy with the tight jeans, cowboy boots and tiny gold earring.

"Ah, Mr..." she looked at her class list, "Sanders. What is so funny? And may I remind you, class, that it is polite to wait until one student has finished with a question before we—"

"Butt in?" he asked innocently, with a smile like a choirboy.

She frowned and bit her lip.

"Peter, the question that Hamlet is presenting is a rhetorical one," she said. "There is no real answer. It demands," here she looked pointedly at the big blond jock, "thought and reflection."

"Ouch," the big one said and wrote something in his notebook.

"Tonight, I am going to pass out our first play, *Romeo and Juliet*, by William Shakespeare. Does everyone know a little bit about the story?" She looked around her class of twenty students.

A hand shot up, lean and tanned.

"I don't know the story," he said. "Can you teach it to me?"

A ripple of laughter ran around the room. Oh, she would teach him a thing or two, all right, before the summer was over.

"Certainly, Mr. Sanders, that's why you're here, isn't it? To learn something about literature and culture and life?"

"Jim," he said.

"What?" she said, noticing the ice blue glints in his eyes.

"Jim, call me Jim. That's my name," he said, and smiled again.

"All right, Jim, and everyone else in the class, here's what I would like you to do. Read the first forty-three pages of the play before we meet next week. That will take us up through the famous balcony scene. Then I want you to write down five questions you have about the play and five facts you learned or liked about it. Then we will pool our questions and focus on concepts."

Heads were bent, fingers grasped pens, and papers shuffled. The room was silent except for the sounds of students writing down the assignment and looking through their copy of the play. One golden head was not bent in writing, it was aimed directly at her. She put on her glasses, ran her hands through her chin-length wavy brown hair and without realizing it, stood up a little straighter. *Chest out, tummy in*, as Mother used to say. For this display of femininity, she got a big wink. Juliet felt a little trickle of moisture slipping between her breasts. *Damn.*

"Now before you go, I'd like you to write down what you personally would like to learn in this class. If you have taken any previous college-level literature courses, please let me know. If you have a word processing program on your phones or devices, please tell me that, too. Please hand in your comments before you leave."

This time everyone settled down to write, including the blond giant.

At the end of class, you-know-who was the last to leave.

"Here's my paper, Mrs. West," he said, like a good schoolboy. He towered over her sitting at the desk. She was a tall woman, five feet ten without shoes, but this man was huge, probably six feet, six inches of lean, tanned muscles. He had chiseled cheekbones, and honey-colored brows framing the bluest eyes she had ever seen on a human.

"Thank you," she said, giving him a glance.

"Can I walk you to your car?" he asked. "It's late and dark and the parking lot is isolated."

"Thank you, but I'm not leaving yet."

"I wouldn't want you to get mugged," he said pleasantly.

"By whom?" she asked. She couldn't resist it.

"Ouch," he said again. "I deserved that, I guess, for acting up in class. Sorry. I've never been to college and I don't know how to act."

She felt a moment of remorse. *Not everyone has had your opportunities, Juliet.*

"You're doing fine," she said. "I'm sorry to be so cross with you, but when you started laughing at Peter quoting *Hamlet* I was ready to ask you to leave."

"Or make me sit in a corner? A time out?" he smiled.

"Something like that," she said, smiling back, in spite of the warning bells in her head.

"I'll behave better next time, I promise," he said. He leaned down and put his hands on the desk. She could see the strength in his long fingers and stared at the golden hairs that sprang out of his knuckles. She exhaled a long breath.

"Are you sure you won't let me walk you outta here? It seems a little warm in this classroom tonight, too much humidity outside, I guess."

"Maybe it's so warm because you're standing so close to me," she said sweetly. "And no, thank you, I can have the security guard see me to my car."

"I'm invading your personal space?" he smiled. "I usually don't get that complaint."

"I'm sure you don't," she agreed. She stared up at him innocently.

"All right, then," he said, "I get the hint. I'll catch you later, Miss teacher lady," and with a devilish smile sauntered out of the room, giving her a good view of his firm backside encased in tight jeans. The silver heels of his boots glinted provocatively.

A dude, she thought to herself and took off her glasses. *When have you ever gotten close to a dude, Juliet? You only know teachers and college kids.*

She looked through her students' papers. She became fascinated with their personal goals and dreams, and lost track of the time. One paper had fringed edges and purple ink.

Dear Teacher, I'm sorry I acted up in class tonight. I didn't mean to laugh, but when that kid started quoting "to be or not to be, that is the question," I couldn't help myself. Some of these college kids are so serious. I never been to college and I never been serious. Well, maybe once or twice. I don't know how to act in school anymore, it's been so long. But I'm gonna try, because you seem like a really nice lady. I wanna tell you I think you're a great teacher. I really liked it tonight when you were talking about Romeo and Juliet and how there are sometimes so many obstacles in the course of true love. And how wealth and social class can ruin a relationship. Or the lack of it. I know what that means. I always had to work for whatever I wanted. I grew up poor, and when I was a kid we slept three in a bed, so I know what it was like to have nothing. Now I'm grown and I ain't—I mean, I'm not poor anymore and I wanna improve myself. I wanna learn things, like how to buy good wine and take a woman to a French restaurant and know what the hell they're talking about on the menu. That's why I'm taking this class. I need culture. I was a Marine, I run my own construction company, I been married and have kids, but I'm not a classy guy. You're gonna help me. Hey, this is only the first class and I feel smarter and more refined already. I'm going home and I'm going to read Romeo and Juliet tonight, the whole play.

Anyway, I wanted to let you know, since you asked us to write about our goals, and Shakespeare, and I know that you are going to be a dynamite teacher this summer.

So, thanks, and you know, and I don't mean to disrespect you, but you're the prettiest teacher I've ever seen.

Juliet West wrinkled her nose. She looked at the essay sitting on top of her laptop and frowned. What the heck was this? Was she going to have another year of strange students with behavioral disorders in her class? She was teaching literature at Thomas Jefferson College, she wasn't a therapist. So why did she get these students who bared their souls to her? She just wanted to teach literature, not be a life coach.

Why was he taking her class? Why would a man with big biceps and a big smile and spiky honey blond hair sit in the back of the class wanting to hear her go on about Shakespeare? With his feet propped up on the chair in front of him wearing macho boots and the rest of him packed into tight jeans and a t-shirt that said Sanders Construction he looked like he could be working for the World Wrestling Federation. She wasn't used to Stone Cold types in her classes. He was attractive and he set her pulses racing. Just when she had embraced her celibacy. This kind of distraction she didn't need during class time.

She looked at her watch. She had been sitting reading their essays for an hour. It was getting late. Time to head home.

Sometimes she went to her yoga studio after class or went to the corner pub to have a glass of wine and talk to her neighbors but tonight she didn't feel like it. She felt too restless, it was better to go home and write to her daughter.

Her daughter, named after the French writer Colette, was in London on vacation with her family.

"Why don't you come to Europe with us?" her daughter had asked.

"I promised to work this summer and besides, the house is going to need a new roof," she had said, with genuine regret.

"I wish Daddy hadn't left you with so many debts," Colette said, "and I hate to think of you here all alone."

"I'm not alone," she had laughed. She liked to keep up the illusion that she had a social life. After her divorce five years ago, she had dated a lot of men, she had been the proverbial kid in the candy shop, sampling a little bit of everything. But no one had really made her feel special or alive and she had declined all offers of lovemaking. But now her dating life was on hold while she got her head together. No more did she go out with just anyone that looked good to her.

She used to meet men at the yoga studio or church and at the park with her granddaughter. She often attracted much younger single men who told her about their lives, bought her dinner and then tried to take her to bed. She had allowed herself to go to dinner and be kissed on the doorstep a couple of times, but she really was the kind of woman who wanted to be in love with a man before she slept with him. She had been faithful to only one partner for twenty-five years and now she was waiting for someone special. But she had been waiting a long time.

For whom she wasn't sure. But she had felt it for a moment tonight. A whisper of interest and desire. How could she feel an attraction to a complete stranger? A cute man, sitting at the back of the class, smiling at all the women and especially at her. She hated this kind of student and this kind of man. He was so secure. She could tell he thought it was funny having a woman tell him what to do.

Oh, he wasn't disrespectful, she could tell that right away. But he bothered her.

"Yes, ma'am I know how to use a dictionary and no, ma'am, I don't have a red pencil and I'll try not to chew my gum so hard, ma'am, right in front of your face," he had said, smiling, tonight in class. Why was he always smiling? He couldn't be happy, could he? When he had asked her tonight if she thought it was possible to fall in love at first sight, like Romeo did with Juliet, she felt her cheeks grow warm.

"Anything is possible," she had said primly. "Particularly when it concerns the human heart." He had just leaned back in his chair and smiled some more.

Her life had never lived up to her literary name. No man had scrambled up her balcony to profess undying love. No man had said to her, *It is the east and Juliet is the sun.* No man had ever defied the stars just to be with her. She was such a romantic.

She believed the stuff she taught her students.

She was shaking her head as she arrived home, pulling up in her battered but solid VW Beetle to her Victorian frame house, painted in pastel shades of lilac, tan and sage. Her young neighbor Beatrice was sitting on the front porch, painting her nails purple.

"How was school today?" Juliet asked her.

"It was all right. But this college might be too hard for me. They look so serious." She was an artist and had magenta hair, toe rings and a pierced navel. She was majoring in art therapy and loved kids.

"Nonsense, you'll do fine. You couldn't stay at the junior college forever. Is your mom back?"

"Tomorrow night. I wish she didn't have to travel for a living."

"I know," Juliet agreed, "but it's a great job and she's so good at training. If you get lonely, dear, come over and talk to me, you know that, anytime."

"Thanks, Juliet," Beatrice laughed. "I like having two Moms. How are your summer classes going?"

"Okay, I think a few of the students might get what I'm talking about right away. And the others are going to have to concentrate," she told her.

"Any cute guys?"

"A few," she said, but she was thinking of one perpetually smiling student who was the most intriguing in her class. What was he up to?

"I should take your class, then," Beatrice said. "No one is interesting in my school."

"Then you can concentrate better and get good grades," Juliet said with a smile. "You have plenty of time for boys later."

Beatrice groaned. "You sound like my mother. I know, guys can be trouble."

"How true," Juliet agreed.

"Have you seen Charles lately?"

"No, I wonder where he's gone off to?" Juliet replied, frowning.

Last semester she had taken a class to the library and a rare book had gone missing. Charles, had been a suspect but it turned out Juliet had been his alibi, as she was giving him a make-up exam. Still, even though the police had cleared him, she had always wondered. There was something a bit odd about Charles.

"You don't really trust him, do you?"

"I wanted to, but his story seemed so rehearsed."

"Let's hope he doesn't come back to school." Beatrice said.

"I know," Juliet agreed. "No more drama, please. I need students who will behave." But would they all behave themselves?

. . .

Juliet took a shower after writing her daughter a lengthy text about the day. She made a cup of chamomile tea and lay on the floor to do her yoga stretches in her studio. The phone rang. "Darn!" she said. Juliet was in the middle of a spinal twist, a yoga exercise that promoted a supple back and no lower back pain, and she had to push herself up from the floor without spilling her tea and reach over to the table. She dropped her cell phone under a stack of yoga mats.

"Hello?" she said, a little out of breath from the stretch and the scramble.

"Mrs. West?"

"Yes? Who is this?" she said, looking at her dark tangle of hair in the mirror.

"It's James Sanders, I'm one of your students. I saw you tonight, remember?"

Her stomach tied up into an instant knot. Of course, she knew that voice. Hot dripping honey. What was the matter with her? Too much ginseng and St. John's Wort? Too much natural estrogen?

"Yes, I remember, how can I help you?"

"I hope I'm not bothering you, 'cause you gave us your e-mail address and phone and said to text you at any time, but I didn't know how long it would take for you to answer me, so I took a chance and called you. I hope you don't mind."

What could she say? "What can I say? I put my number on the syllabus." *Dummy.*

He laughed a little, the sexiest chuckle she had ever heard.

"I'm glad you did," he said in a husky voice that made her breathe a little faster.

"How can I help you?" she repeated. *He was probably too young for her, about forty—whoa—what was she thinking about?*

"Well, I hate to tell you this, but tonight, I've got a date with a lady. A very special lady," he said. "And I wanted to lay on her the stuff you said in class about this flower or bud or Budweiser of love and something about a breath?"

That's nerve, she thought. Calling me to get love lines for your lady. Yet, she was amused.

"*This bud of love, by summer's ripening breath, may prove a beauteous flower when next we meet,*" Juliet recited sweetly into the phone.

"This bud of what? What's ripe? Can you repeat that?" he said anxiously.

Juliet took a deep breath and complied with his request.

"Did you get all that?"

"Yeah, I did, thank you, it's great, I like that line."

"It worked for Juliet," she said.

"Oh, shoot, did a woman say that?" he sounded disappointed.

"Yes, a woman said that line, but really it could work for any hopeful lover."

"Do you think so?" He sounded eager. Her heart lurched.

"Yes, it could. You must have a special lady you're trying to impress."

"Yeah, she's special but she's way too far above me. She's got a lot of dough, she grew up at the country club and I grew up in the trailer park and I'm a builder not a stockbroker. I'm sunk before I begin."

"You must like her a lot if you're going to recite Shakespeare to her."

"I like her, but this is crazy. Her family will think I'm nuts. Just like Romeo."

Just like mine did, Juliet thought, a dagger piercing her chest. They all thought Tony had not been good enough for her.

"Nothing ventured—"

"Nothing gained," he finished. "Hey, I know that one, ma'am. Thanks a lot."

Ma'am! It made her feel ancient.

"My name is Mrs. West. Juliet."

"That's a great name," he said. "Right outta the book you gave us."

"Thank you, I like it."

"I'm sorry calling you up late like this. I hope your husband won't get mad."

"I'm divorced," she said calmly.

"No kidding," he said, and his voice dropped. "That's good to know. Maybe I can try out some of this poetry stuff on you."

"I've got all the poetry I need, thank you," she said stiffly, but he just laughed again.

"Catch you later, Miss teacher lady," he said, and hung up.

Dammit! she thought. Now she would never fall asleep.

She finally went to bed after reading a scene from Hamlet and watching a few minutes of Humphrey Bogart and Ingrid Bergman in Casablanca. Big hats and smoldering cigarettes and tragic love. Now, that was romance. The movie was in black in white, but it was red-hot sizzling passion.

She finally fell asleep after an hour of tossing and turning. Then she had a dream that was a doozy. She was in Jamaica, running along a beach. She was slim and tanned and was wearing a tiny bikini and her muscles were firm and golden brown. She kept looking over her shoulder to see who was chasing her but she couldn't quite make out his face. He looked like Humphrey Bogart and then he turned into a composite of all her students. The students, revolving in psychedelic neon colors, morphed into a Frankenstein's monster wearing jeans and cowboy boots.

The monster turned into a blond bodybuilder with a gold earring who was quoting Romeo as he chased her down the beach. Just as she felt his firm hands around her waist, his hot sweet breath on her neck, she woke up with a groan. She hated sex dreams, she knew what that meant. Her libido was going to reassert itself and cause trouble.

She pulled the sheet up under her nose and through her lashes watched the sunlight streaming through the open window and felt the breeze refresh her face. Outside, birds were singing in her beautiful garden. Hey, maybe life wasn't so bad after all!

The phone rang. Maybe it was her daughter but it was three in the afternoon in England and she usually called late at night.

"Hello?"

"Hi, Mrs. West—Juliet—it's me, Jim Sanders."

She played dumb. "Who?" She asked sweetly into the telephone.

"You know, me, the old guy from your class last night. The one who has been bugging you about poetry and all that stuff it takes to romance a lady."

The nerve.

"Oh yes, I remember you now. But you're not that old, are you?"

"I'm forty-three," he said.

Looks younger, she thought.

"How did the buds of love go over last night?"

That sexy chuckle. "Not too good. She about laughed in my face. Of course, she had drunk a couple of raspberry martinis and was feeling no pain so maybe all those—what did you call them? Shakespearean metaphors—went right over her head."

"I see," Juliet sighed, that's too bad. "Maybe your lady friend doesn't like Shakespeare."

"She's too young for me, anyway," he said. "She was only twenty-five and really silly."

"Really?" Juliet said. "That's younger than my daughter."

"How old is your daughter?"

"She's thirty," Juliet said.

"Wow, you don't look old enough to have a daughter who's thirty."

"I'm fifty-five," Juliet said coolly. *Take that, dude,* she thought.

He whistled, long and low. "Wow, you're really a foxy lady for fifty-five. I never saw a teacher in such buffed condition. I never woulda guessed."

Juliet was pleased at the whistle and then got irritated.

"What was the point of your call, Mr. Sanders? Are we just chatting about age this morning? I have to get up. I have some work to do."

"You're still in bed?" he sounded very intrigued.

"No, I was up, but I'm not dressed yet." Darn, too much information.

"You're not dressed?" his voice dropped, deeper than the Grand Canyon, a caress like angel's wings against naked skin.

What a deep voice you have, Grandpa, she thought. *And what big teeth. The better to eat you with—*

"Not yet, I slept in today. Do you mind?"

"Of course not, you're a teacher. You work hard. And it's Saturday. You have a lot of papers to read," he said. "No, I just wanted to say, that maybe this Shakespeare stuff is too heavy for these ladies, maybe we need to find something more con-tem-po-rary." He said it like a rapper, a Kanye-style construction dude who was built like Atlas.

"Yes? Your point?"

"Well, I got another lady I'm taking out later, and I wanted to try something more modern on her, so I thought I'd call and get your advice."

"Are you going to read basketball scores? Stock market closings? Real estate taxes? That's contemporary information, wouldn't you say?"

"Now that's funny," he said, with another chuckle. "I know I'm a idiot, but you know what I mean. Maybe we can find another poem that makes more sense to a woman."

"What do you mean WE?" she almost, not quite, but almost shouted at him.

That laugh again.

"Please, Miss teacher lady, help me one more time. I just need a little poem to impress a lady tonight."

"How old did you say you were?" she asked him.

"Forty-three."

"I assume you don't have a wife." Got to check, she thought, you never know.

A pause. "I'm not married. My wife died five years ago from breast cancer."

Juliet sucked in her breath. "I'm sorry, I didn't mean to—"

"I know, I act like a cocky son-of-a-gun but really I'm a scared puppy who is trying to forget pain and suffering and all that crap. So, I'm running around reading poetry and taking out young ladies like that will make me happy."

"Do you have children?"

"Two sons, they're twenty-one and twins. Randy and Mike. They're the ones who told me to go back to school. They knew I needed to get some culture, Miss teacher lady."

"Stop calling me that," she said, annoyed. "It makes you sound like you're in eighth grade."

"I am in eighth grade when I'm talking to you. You have some strange effect on me."

Juliet got breathless. "I do?"

"Yeah, it's real weird, but I feel so calm when I talk to you. I feel almost human again."

"I'm glad," she said, feeling weak in the knees. "So, what type of poem are you looking for?"

"Now don't fall down laughing but I got a poem I wrote and I wanted to read it to you and see what you thought."

"Okay," Juliet said, "read it to me."

"Aw, hell, pardon my language, but I can't do that on the phone. Let me stop by for a minute and you can read it yourself."

"Why don't you bring it to school on Tuesday night and I'll read it then," she suggested. She was not used to having students come to her house. She had a strict policy, but still—the thought of him sitting at her kitchen table was tempting.

"But I got a date *tonight*, remember?" he pleaded. "And I need you to help me, I've gotta sound more educated, I'm such a—"

"Diamond in the rough?"

"Something like that," he laughed. "Please, can I bring it by?"

"I'm going to be in and out all day," she said.

"That's okay, I'll just drop by later and see if you're home," he said.

"I don't think it's a good idea," Juliet said.

"Why not?"

"You're my student."

"I'm a big boy, Miss teacher lady," he said softly.

"I—I don't know," she stammered.

"I can behave," he said. "I got good manners."

"All right, but I probably won't be home."

"I'll take that chance," he said.

"How did you get my address?"

A low chuckle. "I'm a good student. I googled you."

She sighed. *Naturally.* "And may I ask how you got another date so quickly with a lady that also likes poetry?"

"Hey, I go with classy ladies," he said in that low, sexy let-me-kiss-you-all-over voice. "But this lady, she's into poetry because she's last night's sister. She wants to do everything the other one does. See you later."

Juliet looked at the phone.

"Right," she said to herself. Absolutely incorrigible. She would most certainly not be at home.

15

CHAPTER TWO

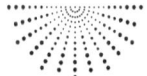

JULIET SAT DOWN AT HER DESK AND TRIED TO WORK ON A SYLLABUS for a class she was creating for next year. She was designing a writing workshop for students at the university, both full-time and continuing-ed ones, like Jim. Jim. What was he up to, now that he had disturbed her morning with his sexy voice and crazy request for love lines? Of course, she couldn't concentrate and nothing sounded right. Maybe it was the bright sunshine or her weird dreams, but she was restless. She closed her laptop and got her yoga bag. Exercise usually helped take some of the jitters away. And the longing.

When she got to the Heavenly Bodies Yoga studio she put on her shorts and t-shirt. She was a tall woman and muscular from years of exercise. She wasn't small, she wore a size fourteen. A very firm size fourteen. Good for staring down fresh students and for lifting boxes of books at home and at school. You had to be tough these days to be a teacher. She had worked for twenty years in an inner-city school, as a Special Education teacher, and she had developed both mental and physical muscles, a sense of humor and when needed, a real attitude.

She lay down on her mat and stretched. Breathe in, breathe

out, still the mind, be at peace. Her friend, Lois, lay down on the mat next to her.

"You're here early today," her friend said to her. She was smaller than Juliet and very slim. She wore her hair in a long blonde ponytail. Her nails were long, tangerine and perfect, each adorned with a sign of the zodiac.

"I couldn't concentrate today, so I thought I'd get out of the house," Juliet said, pulling in her stomach as she looked in the full-length mirrors that covered the walls of the studio.

"Good idea, it's such a beautiful summer day. Any plans tonight?"

"No, I don't," Juliet laughed. "As usual. Maybe a date with an old movie, a bottle of chardonnay and a wedge of brie cheese."

Lois giggled. "I thought you had given up all your evil, bad fattening ways. You said you were going to be good for a while."

"I find lying in bed eating and drinking wine very relaxing," she said. "Not healthy, but relaxing."

"You could burn a lot of calories if you had someone to relax with," Lois suggested.

"You know I am not into the meaningful one-night relationship," Juliet said loftily. "I am looking for true love."

"Right. I hear you. But what is true love anyway? You have to go out once in a while to try to find it. You won't find it at home." Lois looked down at her own figure attired in black yoga pants and a Chicago Cubs t-shirt and sighed. "I've gained seven pounds since I quit working."

"Where?" Juliet looked at her friend. "I don't see one extra ounce on you. And, the burning question is, are you going out with Bill?"

"Yes," she said, "Another real date. He's taking me to the opera. Imagine! I've never been to an opera." She sounded thrilled. "I hope I understand it all. It's in Italian. I only know words like fettuccini and tiramisu."

"You never had time for the opera. You were raising your kids and working damn hard as a lieutenant on the police force. Now that you're retired, you can enjoy new places." Juliet smiled. "And new men."

"Gosh, I wonder if we're going to make love, tonight. It's been two months since we met and he's been very polite."

"That's because you were a cop."

"That's because he's an old-fashioned kind of guy. A Master Sergeant. He was in Iraq. I didn't know there were any gentlemen left on this planet. I had given up hope. Do you know he brings me flowers or a present on every date? Last time he brought me black satin gloves." Lois shivered and rubbed her arms. "Ooh, girl, do they feel good on my arms."

Juliet smiled. "And so, will he. Why don't you make the first move tonight? You can always pull rank. And be the one on top."

Lois' eyes widened and her mouth formed a perfect O.

"You are really bad, you know that?"

"It comes from looking at too many young men at school. Makes my mind go all funny."

"Not your body?"

"I am behaving myself, as you know," Juliet said.

"Why?" Lois asked, watching Juliet execute a perfect downward dog. "I mean I know how you feel about wanting to be in love before you sleep with a man and that's great. But why be so cautious with who you go out with? Why don't you go out with one of your fellow teachers at school?"

Juliet saw a tanned face with blue eyes and a wild grin flash through her mind.

"It's a thought," she said. "Don't you know any nice law enforcement agents? I'm tired of dating men I meet at school or church. Or on-line."

"You should be used to it by now," Lois said, arranging herself in a headstand, "you've been divorced for five years."

"You never get used to meeting strangers," Juliet shrugged,

and finished with a sun salutation. "I always get nervous and then disappointed."

She finished her routine, took a shower, put on khaki pants, a black stretch t-shirt, her new leather slides and looked at herself. She puffed up her chin-length bob, and put on lipstick. She felt thirty-five, not fifty-five. Why not go home and see if anyone showed up? She had a couple of nice bottles of wine in the cellar. French wine. Whoa. She caught herself up again. Is this what she wanted? To flirt outrageously with a man who liked to party and who wanted to date college co-eds? To take a chance with a man and sleep with him and then discover he was boring or that he thought you had too much cellulite on your thighs or crow's feet around your eyes, and he wanted to go bungee jumping? The hell with that. She was going to the movies.

Juliet went to a theater near her home. She loved the movies. Sometimes on a bad Sunday after her divorce she would go and sit through one, two, even three films.

It was an escape and also a way for her to study popular culture. She used the films as references in her classes and as a way to extend the appeal of her writing.

Today she was restless and barely made it through one film. One of her favorite French actresses was seeing three men at once and they all were treating her badly. How could any woman put up with that? She walked out.

Juliet checked her phone. What was her family doing? What was her ex-husband up to? Was he trying to send her any more unpaid bills? Was Tony really happy with his new wife in the suburbs? Did she really care? So many questions, so few reasons to want to know.

This was not a good mood to be in. Why was she supposed to have any answers?

She went home, planning to spend a peaceful night writing and making bread for her weekly visit to her good friend, Paula, in the retirement home on Sunday. Irish soda bread was her specialty. And she wasn't even Irish.

The summer night was cool and fine and she didn't have to put on the air-conditioning. She made two loaves of bread and put them into the oven to bake. Since the kitchen was warming up, she made a cup of coffee and went to sit out on the deck. She had beautiful mosaic pots of coral geraniums, peach roses, purple pansies and in little hand-made ceramic urns she had grown forget-me-nots, basil and lemon balm.

Juliet breathed in the night air. It was clean and fresh and she felt ashamed of herself for being so restless. She should be happy. *But you're alone*, the birds seemed to say as they flew in pairs over her house. *You need a companion*, the two marble angels on her deck whispered to her.

She shook herself. Now her statues were talking to her. She was going crazy. It must have been the movie she had seen today.

The alley behind her house was very clean and neat. Rows of black city-issued garbage dumpsters stood solidly next to wood and chain fences and neatly sided garage doors. Her yard was small, her cedar deck almost reached the alley. From her perch she could see almost anyone at all who was passing or sneaking by.

She took another swallow of coffee and looked at her watch. Another ten minutes and she could take the soda bread out of the oven. She frowned. Was there something moving out there in the dusk? Was it a kid on a bike or a squirrel shaking the branches of the maple tree?

"But soft, what light through yonder window breaks? It is the east and Juliet is the sun."

What was that? She stood up and leaned over the deck, her private balcony. She pinched herself on the arm, above the elbow, a nervous habit from long ago. Then she saw him, standing there, smiling away, holding a book in his hand and wearing glasses.

She smothered a giggle. *Oh no*, she thought, *this can't be happening.* All right, let him have it.

She jumped to her feet and held her hand up to her chest in pretend astonishment.

"What man art thou, thus bescreened in night, so stumblest on my counsel?"

"Thus bescreened in night... stumble... counsel..." She heard the frantic ruffling of pages. *"Arise, fair sun... it is my lady... I am too bold—"*

"I'd say," she rubbed her face and tried not to laugh out loud. Her Romeo was wearing an Undertaker t-shirt.

"Oh, that I were a glove upon that hand, that I might touch that cheek! Who's stumbling on whose counsel? And what's counsel?" he asked up plaintively to Juliet.

She decided to have no pity.

"O Romeo, Romeo, wherefore art thou Romeo?"

"I'm right here, Miss teacher lady, right here in your alley."

"I can see that," she said and continued ruthlessly on. *"Tis but thy name that is my enemy...What's in a name? That which we call a rose, by any other name would smell as sweet."* He was staring at the book, still smiling. She felt a moment of apprehension. *"Romeo, doff thy name, and for thy name, which is no part of thee,"* she hesitated, *"take all myself." Figure that out, baby*, she thought.

He paused and in the streetlight, she could see his bulging biceps, tight jeans, and tattoo on his upper right arm. *What was he, nineteen years old?* That's what he looked like, with the full moon shining like a spotlight behind his head. He was looking in the book and concentrating.

"I take thee at thy word! Call me but love," here he looked up at her and she was pierced by the blue light of his eyes, *"and I'll be new baptized. Henceforth I never will be Romeo."*

She took up her watering can and sprinkled a little over the side of the deck.

"You're baptized. How does it feel? And why are you here?"

"I came around at two, but you weren't home," he said.

"I told you I was busy."

"I was giving an estimate on rehabbing a house over on the next block. The Meyers. Do you know them?"

Fool, she told herself. *You thought he was coming over to see you.*

"Yes, I do. I know them from church. Nice people. I've taught their son."

He was staring at her. "Don't you want to know why I'm here tonight?"

"Giving another estimate?" she asked.

"I came over to see you."

Zounds. Odds bodkins. Bingo.

"I saw you sitting on your deck, looking so pretty and peaceful and I had the book in my Jeep so I couldn't resist."

"Resist what?" she was mesmerized by that light in his eyes.

"Coming around the alley and laying some Romeo and Juliet lines on you. I hope you don't mind."

"I'll get over the shock," she said and took a step back. "Well, it was nice talking to you."

"Wait," he turned a page, *"O wilt thou leave me so unsatisfied?"*

The dog. *"What satisfaction can'st thou have tonight?"* she asked, holding her breath.

"A cup of coffee would be nice," he smiled. "Can I come up, Miss teacher lady?"

She hesitated. Trouble was a-knocking at her door. Or her deck. She could feel it in her bones.

"Come around the front and I'll let you in," she said.

"Why?" he asked. "Let me do a Romeo." He jumped her back gate and then deftly and quickly scrambled up the heavy cedar planks that reinforced the sides of the deck. Up six feet.

He threw one strong leg over the side and then the other. With a graceful leap he was standing beside her.

"Teacher, I'm here." He smiled and she took a little step backwards. *The lion is in my cage,* she thought.

"You did that very well. Were you a cat burglar in another life?"

"No, I was a Marine. We used to spend a lot of time climbing rope walls and mountains of rocks. That's my specialty."

"Yes, I can see that," she said. "Let me get you some coffee."

She walked into her kitchen with him close behind her.

"Hey, what a great smell," he said.

"Oh no, my bread!" She ran to the oven and pulled out two very brown loaves of Irish soda bread.

"I hope I didn't burn it," she said.

"It looks good to me," he said appreciatively. "Do you bake often?"

"Once in a while, when I visit friends, and for my granddaughter. She likes cookies."

"I like cookies," he said, "Miss teacher. I like them a lot." He sat down in an oak captain's chair and smiled.

She poured him a cup of coffee and put a handful of home-baked chocolate chip cookies on a plate in front of him.

His eyes lit up. "Wow, this is living, real coffee and cookies served to me by a beautiful lady."

"What happened to tonight's lady?"

"Excuse me?" he said, too innocently, his eyes bright with mischief.

"What happened to the sister and the contemporary poetry?"

"You were right, they were too young for me. I tried to take her to a antiques show because I was looking for a old mantelpiece for a home I'm rehabbing, but she said she was bored. So, I took her home. I even had a nice quiet roadside inn picked out for dinner. But she don't like the country. Can you believe it?" He grinned at her.

I can't imagine anyone not liking the country. Especially with you for a guide.

"I'm sure it was nothing personal," Juliet said. "She probably has a short attention span."

His shout of laughter warmed her. "Yeah, you're right, when they're too young they can't pay attention. Maybe I should carry some Ritalin around with me when I'm dating these young babes."

"I don't know about that," she said, "maybe a Valium?"

"Hey," he leaned in and winked at her, "I'm not nervous."

But I am, with your tanned self sitting so close to me that I can see the golden hairs on your strong forearms and on your chin.

"No, you don't appear to be nervous," she said, studying him carefully. "You seem very sure of yourself."

"Not always," he said easily. "I've got to find someone a little more mature to go out with. Some of these young girls, they ain't into poetry or antique stuff. They should be going out with my sons."

She stirred more cream into her coffee and looked at him. He didn't look the least bit daunted by anybody's age.

"Maybe the next lady will like Shakespeare. And your poems. You said you wrote one, didn't you? And you wanted to read it to me?"

"I don't know if I can read it to you. I'd feel like a dork. You're so classy and smart and I'm just a rough guy," he said.

"You don't look so rough to me."

"I'm rough, I'm a animal. After Barbara died, I really turned into a caveman."

"Your wife?"

"Yeah, I went really insane for a while."

"How do you mean?"

"I didn't care how I looked or what I ate and the boys were only sixteen and I was trying to be both mother and father and not get drunk or crazy because I was so lost without her, and I pulled way into myself. Built a fort and started hiding, if you know what I mean."

"I know all about hiding," she said.

"Okay, you do know that feeling of being all alone and not

caring if you ever see another human being again. So, I worked a hell of a lot and made money and tried to be there for the boys and I even went to a fancy head doctor—"

"A psychiatrist?"

"Yeah, and he gave me Prozac and it kept me from getting real psycho, but sometimes I would send the boys over to Grandma's and I would get real drunk and drive up to Wisconsin and look at the girls dancing and throw money around and just act stupid." He paused. "Tired of me, yet?"

"No, I'm fascinated," she said. "Go on."

"That's all, really. After a couple of years, I settled down a little and got the boys into college and tried to date some real women, not strippers I met at clubs 'cause they didn't ask me questions, and now I'm tryin' to get some culture."

She raised her eyebrows in disbelief.

"I see that look," he said. "Why? Because my sons told me to. Go back to school, Dad, learn something new. Forget about being a Marine and a builder and guy who makes a lotta money by sweating and bossing people around and wearing a hard hat."

"But Shakespeare?"

"Hey, Mrs. Juliet West, one of the wild, wild Wests, I'm thinking. I like Shakespeare."

They stared at each other. She licked her lips nervously. He was staring at her with a dark, primitive look on his face, a look she had only seen on other women's men.

"How about your poem?" she said at last. He put his coffee cup down with a bang. They both looked surprised at the noise. He shrugged one massive shoulder.

"Another time. I gotta work on it some more. I need to listen to you talk more in class about tempo and metaphors and the beauty of the human soul and then I'll see what happens."

She jumped up and went over to the coffee pot. Was he after her or maybe he was just after her mind? Maybe he just wanted to feel more connected with his intellectual side. Maybe he was looking for a free therapy session, she told herself. She poured them both more coffee and tried not to look into his eyes.

"Thank you," he said politely and waited for her to sit down before he took a sip.

She glanced at the tattoo on his arm. A small red rose with two stars around it.

"You're looking at my arm," he said.

"Yes, it's pretty for a tattoo. Did you get it when you were a Marine?"

"Nope, I got it five years ago, right after Barbara died. I woke up one morning in my truck with a hangover and bottle of tequila at my feet and this." He pointed to his arm. "The rose is for my wife, and the stars are my sons. They're twins, my sons."

"I guess you do have the soul of a poet," she said, wanting to cry. "I hate tattoos as a rule, but that's lovely. It represents your past and your present."

He leaned over in his seat. He was nearly touching her.

"How about my future?" he said softly, and quickly kissed her mouth.

She felt the electric current run through her veins. She was shocked by the warmth and the softness of his lips. She wanted to shout, it felt so good. She got up swiftly, too fast and knocked over a vase on the table. The water pooled around their coffee cups.

"I'm a teacher, not a curandera or the psychic hotline," she said at last, coldly. "I can't answer your question."

She mopped up the mess. He stood up and looked at her.

"Sorry for that. I shouldn't have kissed you. I dunno what came over me. But I am so attracted to your sweetness." She stared at him open-mouthed. "Now you're mad at me."

"Maybe it was just the Shakespeare," she said. "Or memories."

"Forgive me?" he did look anxious for once.

"Forgiven, but don't do it again."

"Yes, Miss teacher lady." He winked seductively. "I'll wait until I'm asked."

He smiled and wandered into the living room. She followed him, arms wrapped around herself, warily watching him looking at the pictures on the piano, the walls and the coffee table.

"Your daughter?"

"Yes, that's Colette, her husband Paul, and their daughter, Angelica."

"Nice looking family. She looks like you."

"My daughter?" she was pleased to hear that.

"Both the girls," he said. "They both have that mystical look about them. Like a lady from King Arthur or Robin Hood. So do you. In this light, you could be Juliet, you look so young and so pretty."

Liar, she thought, but she smiled and said, "Thank you. You know how to flatter a woman."

"This ain't, I mean this isn't flattery. God, I talk bad. This is ridiculous."

"What is?"

"Tryin' to go to college so I can talk good and know more about books and music and not be such a dumb jock knucklehead. I dunno if it's gonna work."

"You've only come to one class," she said softly. "Don't decide right now."

He smiled and she felt her knees buckle. "Okay, I won't, Miss teacher lady. I'm going to come two nights a week and really learn something. I'm gonna get educated and I'm gonna get refined. You're gonna help me."

He picked up another picture off the piano.

"Your husband?"

"My ex," she said.

"What was his story?" Jim asked her.

"He liked to bet on horses and didn't pay his bills."

"Ouch. Not good for a hard-working teacher lady."

"No, not good at all."

"So, you unloaded him, right?"

"Something like that. It was hard but I paid off our debts and moved on."

"I bet it was hard. I hate owing money, we owed plenty when I was a kid. I know what you need, you need cheering up. Let me take you out tonight, we can see the world," he snapped his fingers, "do the town. Okay? I know a great bar with oysters and Cajun music and the best margaritas."

She stared at him. She could imagine doing a slow dance with this urban cowboy. He could envelope her in a big bear hug and she wouldn't even have to move her feet. Should she go out and say the hell with being good?

He took her silence for agreement.

"Let me just make a call," he said and whipped out his cell phone. "Gotta change some plans."

What plans, she thought? *Another date? Was he a cowboy-booted Casanova?* What was she getting into?

"No, I can't tonight," she said firmly. "I'm not drinking today or going out." He shut off the phone. "Why not?" he looked puzzled. "Are you grounded or something? Won't Mom let you go out tonight, little girl?"

CHAPTER THREE

"I'M IN TRAINING," SHE SAID. "I'VE PUT MYSELF ON THE WAGON."

"What wagon? In training for what? The Shakespeare Olympics?" he laughed and she had to admit, he was very handsome and appealing when he smiled. She could imagine that smile in a candlelit bedroom. *Watch it*, she told herself.

"I'm teaching my first yoga class in two weeks," she said.

His eyes lit up, hunks of blue ice directed at her.

"Really? Are you gonna do all sorts of cool poses? You know, dogs and swans and all that good stuff? Can I come and watch?"

"Yes, to cool poses," she said, making a face at his adolescent enthusiasm. "No, to your coming to watch. I'm teaching this class in an assisted living facility. My class will be senior citizens and some of the staff."

"I'd still like to see that," he said, following her back into the kitchen. "I used to do a bit of weightlifting in the Marines. Check this out."

Juliet felt her heart racing as he flexed his biceps and then his chest muscles and held himself in a total muscleman pose. He raised his arms, he stuck out his long, firm legs and he grunted.

"How's this?" he asked and turned around, hunching up his

shoulders to display rock hard neck and back muscles. Then he had the nerve to squat down in a posture that emphasized his tight, firm buns.

Juliet took a quick sip of water. "Great," she said. She was burning up. "You look like you've kept up with the weights since the Marines."

He turned around and smiled, unaware of how his lean body and bright, sexy smile had caused her blood pressure to rocket off the charts.

"Only in the garage once in a while. I've kept fit by working. I don't just supervise my workers. I work with them. That's the only way to keep quality high and prices reasonable."

"You should teach a class," Juliet said.

"In what?" He came up close to her. She could smell his lemon-scented cologne. "Weightlifting? Construction? Picking up ladies?"

She took a step back.

"How about marketing? You are very good at promoting yourself."

He laughed again. "I'd like that, Miss teacher lady. But only if you were in my class. I'd like to teach you."

"Teach me what?" she asked. He really was ridiculous.

"Lots of things," he said. "How about it?" he said. "I could be your personal trainer and your manager." He leaned in again. "I'd like to manage you."

Every word out of his mouth dripped sex. How could he infuse such ordinary phrases with such charged up sexuality? She wished she could bottle and sell his energy. Then she would pay off her debts.

"I have a yoga coach, but thanks for asking," she said politely and pushed open the kitchen door. He followed her outside. She was aware of his scent, the night air, his strength behind her. She felt a momentary weakness. Why not go out? Why not forget the seriousness of life for just one evening?

"Let's make a deal, teacher," he said, looking at her house.

"What deal?" she said, instantly wary.

"You help me with poetry and I'll help you with your house. I could come over and fix this up for you. You don't want it to start rotting this winter." On the side of the house, several pieces of old wood shingle were slowly, elegantly crumbling away.

It was just a small area of her house but a repair that screamed *pay money, Juliet and fix me up! Before the termites arrive. And the melting snow seeps in.*

"Well, I don't know, that's nice of you to offer, but I couldn't really afford your prices."

"Now how do you know my prices, young lady?" he asked with a smile. "I can work very cheaply with the right incentives."

"If you think you are going to get me into bed with an offer to fix up my house, you are wrong," she said coldly.

"And you are wrong, Miss teacher lady," he said, his smile fading. "You got a dirty mind. I just want to help you because I like you and you look like you need some help around here. I know what it costs to fix things in these old houses. That's how I make my money, remember?"

"I remember," she said. "I'm sorry for jumping to conclusions."

"That's okay, I'm used to pretty women insulting me. I guess they get nervous when they're around me."

"I'm not nervous," she said indignantly.

"Okay, then," he leaned up against the deck. "Show me some of your yoga positions that you are going to teach to the old folks."

"Here?" she was stunned.

"I'm not asking you to jump out of a cake honey," he said, and led her to the middle of the deck. "I just want to see one of your routines."

"No, I can't, not here in front of you," she said. She wasn't sure she was ready to let her guard down in front of him.

"How can you be a yoga teacher if you won't demonstrate in front of me?" he asked, with a puzzled grin.

"I can do it in front of a large group because I don't have to focus on one face," she said defensively. "But in front of you— it would be like doing—"

"The dance of the seven veils?" he smirked. "Like Salome?"

"For a man who says he doesn't know anything about culture, you seem to know a lot more that you give yourself credit for," she said coldly.

"Hey, I've seen that old movie, my Grandmaw loved Rita Hayworth. I watched a lotta cool stuff with her, when she was babysitting. The Bible according to Hollywood. I'm not totally clueless."

"I never said you were," she said.

"So, are you going to do a lotus for me?" He stepped in close.

Do it, she thought, show off a little and watch him squirm. He smiled and his eyes widened, he was so close she could see that his pupils had become large, dangerous black dots in an electric blue sea.

Her psychology classes told her that when men got excited their pupils get bigger. He's enjoying this way too much, she told herself.

He took her hand. "Come on, honey, don't be shy." He grabbed her hands and started to raise her arms above her head. She was aware of her bosom only inches away from his chest. "One tiny little pose?"

She pulled her hands down with an abrupt yank and pushed him away with all her strength. He rocked back on his feet, off balance for a moment. His eyes widened again in what looked like a jolt of extra pupil-widening shock and then she realized, pleasure. He probably likes to wrestle with a woman, she thought. It probably turns him on.

"I hope I didn't shove you too hard," she said sweetly. "But you really have to learn how to give people their space."

"Should I write *I must not touch the teacher* a hundred times?" he asked, rubbing his chest. "You got strong hands. Crazy."

"It must be the moon that makes me act so crazy, I swear I'm not myself tonight," she sighed insincerely.

"Oh lady, swear not by the moon... that monthly changes in her circled orb, lest that thy love prove likewise variable."

Out of Tarzan, these wondrous words of beauty.

She stared at him.

"You've learned an awful lot in one class, Mr. Sanders," she said coolly. "Are you sure you're not here to check up on me?"

"How do you mean?" he asked her.

"Maybe you're from the department of accountability and you're trying to check up on professors in the college. You know, trying to see if they act professionally."

Well, she had failed most nobly, with her taking a sock at him.

"What a great idea," he said, "especially if they all look like you, Juliet. But you're wrong," he said, and got close to her again, "I'm not accountable at all, oh no, not at all for my actions. Especially when I see something I like." He took her hand and raised it to his lips. "Please forgive me for acting out of line just now."

She felt burned by his warm, soft lips. She couldn't move.

"How do you remember so much of the dialogue from Romeo and Juliet in so little time? I passed out the play two days ago." She couldn't believe he was for real.

"I remember plenty, I've got one of those photographic memories, it was a great help in the Marines and in business. I don't even have to carry a notebook or a laptop or a bunch of bills in my car. I always remember what people said and what they owe me. Not for long, but for a couple of weeks or so. It's exceptional short-term memory. Very handy."

"Yes, I'm sure. For phone numbers and the names of all the sisters you're trying to date."

He chuckled. "Are you jealous?"

"Of course not!" she said, pulling her hand away. "Don't be ridiculous. With that kind of memory, you should be an actor. It would be easy with your looks and nerve and memory."

"Why, thank you ma'am," he drawled, "but you see, I have one problem."

"What's that," she said, waiting to hear about his unfulfilled libido.

"I don't know what the hell it all means. What's an orb? Why do they swear so much, Romeo and Juliet? I need you to explain it to me." He took her hand again. "You see we could help each other. I could help you with your poses and you could help me learn about poetry, what it all means."

"I'll think about it," she said, wanting to feel the touch of his lips on her hand again.

"We could be a great team," he said. "I just need a little refinement." He took her hand again and gently squeezed her fingers. She shivered a little from his touch.

"So, what about it? Want to go out tonight?" He looked so sure of himself. She felt his raw energy wash over her and her self-control was getting shipwrecked. Had she totally lost it?

"Thank you, but I don't want to go sit in a bar."

"We can go somewhere without smoke or alcohol. You can drink ginger ale."

"No, thank you, I'm going to stay home."

"We can stay here," he smiled.

"I'm going to go to bed early."

"Alone?"

"That's none of your business."

He picked up his book from the table.

"I get it, the brush off, the slip, the counterfeit, like Mercutio called it. I thought you liked me."

"I do like you," Juliet said with exasperation, "but I told you; I don't go out with my students."

"I'm not a student, I'm all grown up." His eyes looked her up and down, taking in her dark, face-framing hair, full breasts and pink toenails. She blushed.

"You're still a student to me," she said with an air of finality.

"If I quit the class, will you go out with me then?"

She walked over to the deck's edge. "Don't quit the class, it will be good for you. Quit my class, if you like and take it with another teacher, but don't quit. It would be a shame not to put that good a memory to work."

"Why, Miss teacher lady, I do believe you care after all," he said softly behind her.

"Of course, I care about all my students," she said lightly. "The fact that you're there in class at all shows you do want to improve yourself and learn something about literature."

He smiled at her and shook his head.

"You don't get it, you don't get it at all," he said. "I'm taking your class because I want to meet a better class of chicks."

Now she was furious. "How will you ever acquire the culture you said you so badly need if you talk like that about—chicks? Chicks?" her voice rose a few decibels. "That's such a fifties kind of word."

"I always liked Elvis," he said and winked at her. "And I'm just an ignorant farm boy. My family moved to Chicago from downstate a long time ago."

"That's very interesting, but you'd better go," she said.

"Before you show me the door?" he looked over the side of the deck.

"You can use the front door," she said coolly. "Follow me."

"Nope, I'll go the way I came. I'm sorry I wasted your time."

"It wasn't a waste," she said, immediately wanting him to stay. "We at least know where we stand."

"We do?" he said, throwing one leg over the railing surrounding the deck. He smiled at her. "Then you're a hell of a lot smarter than I am, Miss Juliet, 'cause I'd say we are both attracted to each other and going about it the wrong way. At least

I am," he said, "I'm acting like a high school boy. But when I get around you, I get nervous."

"You do?" she said. Now she wanted him, wanted him like hell. She wanted to reach out and pull him off the fence and into her arms. *Watch it, Juliet,* she told herself. *Calm down.*

He opened the book, straddling the fence, an urban Romeo in boots and jeans and a Rolex watch.

"I'm not the kind that gives up so easily," he said in a dangerously serious voice.

She exhaled. The night was growing warmer and she was getting weaker.

"This bud of love by summer's ripening breath may prove a beauteous flower when next we meet," he read to her.

"You said that beautifully," she said.

He put the book in his back pocket and braced his hands on the railing.

"So, there's hope for me?"

"Of course," she said innocently. "You can acquire culture and polish at any age."

"You're going to shine me up?" he asked.

She thought of rubbing his hard, brown, lean body until her hands ached. "Something like that. A mental shine."

"Right," he said, "I like that idea."

"I wish you'd leave the right way."

"No thanks, I'll leave the way I came; in the dark, in the alley, all alone."

"Sounds like poetry," she said.

He dropped to the ground softly.

"You're having a good effect on me already, teacher," he said. She saw his blond hair below her. He was dangerous because he was not afraid of her. She felt a tinge of panic. "Catch you later." He was disappearing into the night.

"James!" she called over the side.

He turned back. "What's the matter? Are you okay?" He came back swiftly and stared up at her.

"I'm okay," she breathed at last.

"Are you sure?"

"Yes."

"Why did you call me back?"

"I forget," she said.

"Then I'll hang around here until you remember."

"No, don't, that's silly. I feel like a fool."

"Juliet called Romeo back," he said softly. "Balcony scene. You're very pretty in the moonlight. I feel real good talking to you. Real peaceful like."

"Me, too," she said. "You have an interesting philosophy about life. I don't think I've ever met anyone like you."

"That's good," he said. "I like being unique."

"You're unique, all right," she said. She looked up at the moon and shivered. "Go home, James and be careful. The alleys are so dark."

"I'll be careful but I won't go home," he said. "It's way too early for a pirate like me to go home." He grabbed her hand and again kissed it swiftly, then dropped to the ground.

"Good night, teacher. *Parting is such sweet sorrow—*"

"*That I shall say good night, 'til it be morrow,*" she finished. Why did she let him go?

He went out the gate into the alley and turned, giving her a wave. In the alley lights she could see him walking away, talking into his cell phone.

CHAPTER FOUR

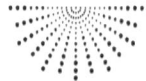

"Tonight, class, we are going to talk about what we read over the weekend. Did everyone bring their book?"

Juliet looked around the room and got affirmative nods in reply. It was a warm night and the air-conditioning in the school didn't seem to be kicking in very well. She felt a little moist under the arms and wiped away a tiny bead of sweat from her brow, with her signature lace handkerchief. She always carried one in her purse; lace and linen were the stuff of poets, right?

Also, the stuff of poetry were hand-tooled boots, tangy, citrus cologne, golden earrings and pirates. And she was looking at one, a big, blond pirate sitting in the back of her class, feet up, head way back, wearing sunglasses. He looked like an urban pirate, all muscle and brawn, ready to throw any of these lovely college girls over his shoulder and make a fast run for his ship.

Quit it, Juliet, she told herself. *You're getting fanciful and you've got two hours ahead of you.*

"All right class, I put together a short question sheet for you to use. See if you can answer these questions and we'll discuss them in about ten minutes? I want to know how well you absorbed what you read."

"Absorbed like suntan lotion?" asked the blond hunk with a grin.

Some of the class laughed, she frowned. She walked resolutely to the back of the room, hand on hip, a wry expression on her own tanned face. She looked him up and down. He was slouched back in his chair, looking weary.

"Yes, absorbed like lotion, or like too many beers in a tired body," she said without mercy.

"Ouch," he said with a faint smile. "I was overserved last night."

"At a poetry slam?" she asked him innocently.

He frowned. "The only thing slamming is my head. I'm sorry about the sunglasses," he said, lifting the Ray-Bans up and looking at her with a faded but very virile look, "but my head is killing me."

"That's all right," she said, "you make a very attractive vampire."

The class laughed, he groaned, and she went back to work.

"If I was Romeo, I would have never agreed to marry Juliet," said a young man in black with a shaved head and nose-ring. "It was way too dangerous."

"Yes, but in their society, there was no way for them ever to meet outside the confines of their homes without the marriage to protect them. She just couldn't go out to the mall or a bar and wait around for him. Church was the only place a woman of her class could go to without the protection of her family around her. This was 1400 in Italy," Juliet smiled, "I know it seems like the dark ages to you, but really it was for her own safety. There were too many bandits and troublemakers on the streets back then. Women had to watch their virtue, it was as important as their dowry."

Heads were bent and notes were being taken at a furious pace. A hand shot up in the back of the room.

"It's pretty dangerous now, teacher, for women," the pirate

said. "You never know what you're going to find on the street or in a tavern these days. Guys are rough."

"Do you speak from personal experience, Mr. Sanders," she asked sweetly, "or are you speaking for all of your sex, generally?"

"Ma'am, I don't know what the heck generally means but I do know men. If you give them an inch, they'll take a mile," he smiled.

She was annoyed. "You mean, they will behave like Romeo, climbing up garden walls unannounced and uninvited?"

He smiled and pushed up his sunglasses for a moment. "Something like that. When a man is in love with a woman, he will follow her everywhere."

"You mean stalk her?" asked a young woman in the front.

"No, no, I mean follow her like Romeo did, wandering around, drinking beers or ale or whatever they did then, talking to your buddies, getting blasted, wishing you were with her, and going about it the wrong way."

Juliet was now amused. "And what is the right way?"

"I don't know," he said, running his hands through his blond hair that stuck up like a rock star. "I suppose he should have gotten the priest or the friar to marry them right away and then gotten that Friar Laurence dude and the whole damn monastery to go over to her father's and say, hey, I just married your daughter, and there's nothing that you can do about it, so let's have a big party and bury the hatchet!" He smiled triumphantly, pleased with himself.

"Well, that would have been more sensible but remember, Romeo was only sixteen and teenagers don't always think logically," she said. "But I like your scenario."

"How would you go about it today?" a redhead in a tight t-shirt asked James.

He smiled and she knew she had lost her class for an interlude.

"Well, I would go buy flowers and champagne and maybe a

little diamond necklace in the shape of a heart and I'd write a poem on red velvet paper and white ink, that said, 'please go out with me tonight, I want to show you the stars,' or something like that, and then I'd get a nice quiet table in a dark corner of a great restaurant—and I would romance her. Until she agreed to marry me."

The redhead sighed a little. "Sounds good to me."

He winked and put his dark glasses back on. He turned his dark glance on Juliet.

"Sorry, Mrs. West, but I talk too much."

"Of course not, your remarks were very interesting," she said, ignoring his grin aimed straight at her. "But let's get back to question number four."

The minutes ticked by. Juliet worked hard to get her class to think and make comparisons between the past and the present. Her pirate with the cowboy boots sat quietly, making an occasional note, popping gum in his mouth and acting subdued.

Thank goodness for that.

"For Thursday night, please read the next twenty-eight pages, that will take us up through the wedding of Romeo and Juliet and the fight between the Montagues and the Capulets resulting in Tybalt and Mercutio's deaths. I have a question sheet for you to take home, tonight. It will help you with your reading."

Another hand shot up.

"This is like gangs, right?" said the young man with the shaved head, "I mean, these people are like street gangs, except it's your castle and my castle and the wrong side of the moat or whatever."

The class laughed; a hit had been made.

Juliet laughed, too. "You're right, Carlos, that was a very astute observation. The enmity between the Montagues and the Capulets had gone on for generations. The parents were involved, too. Romeo and his friends had learned to hate. We need to consider what Shakespeare is trying to say about the community at that time." Everyone was looking at her intently, including the handsome vampire with the dark glasses. "This is not just about art and love but about social conditions. Go home and think about that while you read."

Her class exited, talking about gangs and sociology. Juliet was pleased she had made an impression and a connection. She stood at her desk, passing out homework and answering questions. She felt a connection herself, tonight. Teaching was a joy, especially when it was going well. The students left, all except one, sitting in the back of the classroom.

She picked up a paper. "Your homework, Mr. Sanders," she said, holding it out in his direction. "You have two days to work on it, if you can ever get your eyes to focus."

"Mercy, Miss teacher lady, don't be so mean," he groaned. "I've got such a terrible hangover." He unfolded his height from the chair and slowly moved across the room. The nearer he got, the hotter she became. Heavens, she was supposed to be through with hot flashes by now, wasn't she?

"You got drunk on a Monday night?" she asked primly.

He laughed. "Sorry, Miss Schoolmarm, but us big dumb construction jocks don't worry about what night it is when we go out." He plopped down in a plastic chair next to her desk, and propped his head on his big, strong hands. She fought down the urge to run her fingers through his soft, spiky blond hair. He was a blond Elvis, and she was all shook up.

"It was Monday," she repeated.

"I know, Miss Teacher, but some buddies of mine from the Marines showed up, I hadn't seen them in ten years and I had to take them out and show them around, didn't I? Hell, we was just kids back then and we was so scared and so happy that we didn't get our heads blown off that we got a strong bond between us all. Can you understand that?"

He tore off his sunglasses and looked at her appealingly. Her heart melted. *Gee, he was gorgeous. Why did she refuse to go out with him Saturday night?* She knew why. She was trying to protect herself.

"I understand, loyalty and friendship," she said, annoyed. "I'm not as cold as you think."

He reached over and took her hand.

"I never said you were cold, Miss Juliet," he murmured, staring her in the face. "Just a little nervous, that's all."

She pulled her hand away. "I'm not nervous," she said strongly. "You have the wrong idea about me, dear one. I'm not afraid of you at all."

"I know, you used to teach in the inner city and you live alone and you teach yoga and you're a real dynamite kinda lady," he smiled. "Go out with me, tonight, Juliet, please?" he looked so sincere. "Pretty please?"

"You seem to know a lot about me," she said, feeling like he had intruded on her private space.

"I'm very interested in you," he said. "And you have a great rep. I asked at the registrar's office who the best teacher was in this school and they said it was you."

"Liar," she said to him, feeling flushed but pleased. "They don't tell you that in the office."

He laughed, always at ease. "Okay, but they did tell me how you helped a kid last year and how you were something of an investigator."

"Are you referring to the missing book? I didn't do very well with that disaster."

"Nothing was ever proved, right?"

"No, but I still wonder if one of my students figured out how to go back to the library and steal it."

"Who was the student?"

"He was a rich kid with a lot of privilege and also a learning disability. I was helping him."

"And what happened?" Jim asked.

"He had asked me a lot of questions about the security in the library. I thought he was just intrigued by technology. Then the book went missing."

"And was it him?"

"I turned out to be his alibi," she said. "But I always wondered if he had an accomplice."

"Where is he now, this kid?"

"I don't know," she said. "He's not in the summer session, nor did he sign up for the fall semester."

"Maybe it's better that he's gone," Jim said, pushing his glasses up on his head again. His eyes, bright blue with pink rims, were focused on her.

"Because you think he's dangerous?" she said.

"Don't you?" he asked.

"Not really," she said. "Nothing was ever proven. He doesn't need money, he has plenty."

"Many people who steal do it for the thrill," he said, with a frown.

"I hope you're wrong," she said, mesmerized by his blue eyes that were focused on her tanned, soft face with deep brown eyes and high cheekbones.

"Me too," he said with a smile. She felt her heart beating as he looked her up and down. "How about it, go out with me tonight, Juliet? Just one little, tiny beer?" He leaned in closer and raised a tanned finger. "Hmm? Just one?"

"Haven't you had enough already?" she asked him.

"Then let's not go for a drink," he said. "Let's go to a fancy coffee bar, get a latte or a mocha-chino or whatever you upscale urban professionals drink."

"I'm not upscale," she said. "I'm a teacher in a small college living in a house that needs a lot of work. I teach literature, I'm not a stockbroker or a lawyer."

"Thank God for that," he sighed. "I mean I might have fallen in love with you anyway, but I don't know, you might have had a bigger attitude and I might have been afraid. But poetry and

Shakespeare and *but soft what light through yonder window breaks?* That I can really warm up to in a woman."

"I'm so glad that you're happy with me," she said coolly, but she was in shock. *Had he just said he was in love with her? Ignore that, Juliet or you will be in trouble, for sure.*

"Tonight, go out with me, help me sober up a little? Please?"

She was tempted, soooooo tempted.

"No, I'm going home, I'm tired, I didn't sleep well last night, I was worried about my daughter being in Europe with her husband and my granddaughter. Terrorist attacks—too many are happening. I had a dream there was a problem and they couldn't get home."

"Where are they travelling?" he asked.

"England and Scotland," she said.

"Let's hope it stays peaceful around there," he said. "There is a lot of trouble in the world these days. She'll be okay. Think positively. Go out with me. I'll be your distraction and your team leader." He winked at her.

"Distraction? What are you," she demanded, "a life coach?"

"No, ma'am, I'm just a dumb old farm boy trying to acquire some polish for a new life," he said with an innocent choirboy smile.

"And I'm supposed to help by watching you drink cappuccino, I suppose?" she inquired archly. Damn, when he looked at her, she could feel a tiny bead of sweat trickling down her back, pushing against her black linen blouse.

"I just wanted a friend," he said sadly. "I wasn't up to any tricks," he raised his hand, "I swear to—"

"Oh, swear not by the moon... the inconstant moon," she said feeling devilish, *"lest that thy love prove likewise variable.* Go home, Mr. Sanders," she said, "you look exhausted and not fit company for any lady. Maybe another time."

"Okay, I get it," he said with a rueful grin. "I'm a alley cat with a mangy two-day beard and you don't wanna get close to me."

Oh, but I do, she thought. *Very close.* But it wouldn't be good for her mental health or her career. She was going to apply for the head of the department when the dean retired this year. She must act proper and well-behaved, right? Dating one of her students, even a forty-three-year-old one wouldn't help her get the position.

"Go home," she said kindly. "Go to sleep for a while. You'll feel better in the morning. Did you even sleep at all last night?"

He smiled again. "No, we closed the last bar and went right out for breakfast. And naturally, I had to work today. I'm surprised I didn't drop a drill on my foot." He leaned in one last time. She could smell his citrus cologne and see the golden stubble on his chin. "Don't you feel sorry for me even a little bit, Miss teacher lady?"

She raised a hand and pushed away a firm, hard chest. Her hand felt on fire.

"No, I don't feel sorry for you," she said, keeping a grip on her nerves. "You had a good time and now you must repent."

"Ouch," he said and ambled to the door. "Don't stay here all night," he said to her, "it isn't safe. These buildings are very quiet and isolated." His look of concern thrilled her.

"Thank you, but I'm perfectly fine here."

"Just be careful," he warned. "Goodnight."

"Bye," she said. *Parting is such sweet sorrow that I shall say goodbye 'til it be morrow,* she thought. But he was already gone, and she was alone.

She finished her work, made a few notes, sent a couple of emails and packed up to go home. The hallways were quiet and solitary, although well-lit. She could see her face reflected in the glass of the classroom doors. A serious, tall voluptuous woman with dark wavy hair and big brown eyes, still not ashamed of feeling passion or wonder. She wore a long black linen skirt and shirt, and silver jewelry adorned her ears, fingers and wrists. She wore many bracelets, Native American and Mexican hand-made bangles and they clinked and jingled musically as she walked. With her leather knapsack slung over her shoulder, she looked forty-five instead of fifty-five and she felt still young and unfulfilled.

What do you really want, Juliet? Another marriage, to become the head of the department, how about a literary odyssey around the world? She could write a story in every country. Or why not sell her crumbling old house and buy a chic condo along the lakefront? She liked to walk and bicycle and there were more single people over that way. Both men and women. She always liked to make new friends.

She was deep in thought about life changes and choices. She was not paying particular attention to the hallways that fanned out from the main corridor. Why should she? She had walked this way hundreds of times before at all hours.

When the hands grabbed her from behind, she thought, *I'm going to be mugged, after all these years of safety.* She was pushed into an empty classroom and fell over a chair. She sat sprawled in the dark, panting in fear, her hands raised above her, waiting for an attack.

CHAPTER FIVE

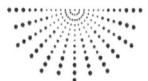

"Who's there?" she asked, fighting for composure. "Who are you and what do you want?"

The light flicked on and she blinked as the cold, cruel fluorescent lighting washed over her and her abductor.

A short, thin, young man wearing preppy style clothes stood in front of her blocking the door. Wire-rimmed glasses framed cool grey eyes. He wore loafers and on his wrist, an expensive gold watch. His hair was very light and baby fine. He looked innocent, yet there was wiry strength that emanated from his tense body.

She got up slowly, brushing dust from her clothes. "Charles, how you scared me."

"Sorry about that. I'm back," he said, smiling. "Did you miss me?"

She stared at him. The look on his face made her skin crawl. Was he drunk or high?

"Where have you been?" she asked calmly.

"I was visiting a rich auntie in New York," he shrugged. "The family wanted to get rid of me for a while. They don't know I'm back yet." He giggled. "I need another book."

"Oh, Charles," she sighed, "then it was you. That book was a very valuable donation to our college. How did you do it?"

"It was easy. I managed to lift the key off the doofus librarian when you brought us in there and made a quick wax copy. And then put it back in his pocket before the end of the day."

"How did you learn to be so devious?" she was in shock.

"Comes naturally," he boasted. "Even though everyone said I had ADHD and a personality disorder, and gave me lots of meds when I was a kid to calm me down, I learned a few things along the way."

"You had—have a lot of potential, Charles. I knew that when I met you in grammar school."

"Yes, we go back a long way," he remarked, leaning against the door. "Fifth grade? How come you left my school?"

"I got a Master's in Literature and decided to try my hand at college classes. After so many years in elementary school, I wanted a challenge."

"I love challenges," he said. "We have a lot in common."

"May I ask, how did you get the book out of the library if I was giving you a test?" This the police had asked her over and over.

"Ah, that's for me to know and for you to find out," he taunted her.

"Did you have an accomplice?" she asked.

"I didn't need any help," Charles smirked. "I wore a disguise, a hoodie and different glasses, when I went back and took the book. You adults don't know everything. What matters now is that I need cash and you're going to help me get some."

"By stealing another book?" she demanded.

"Maybe," he looked at his hands and smiled.

Juliet felt a pang of fear.

What else could he possibly want to steal?

"I think you should turn yourself into the police," she said. "Return the book."

"Can't," he said. "I sold it. And besides, I am not going to jail. No way. If you go and report me, I'm just going to say you've been sexually harassing me and that's why I disappeared in the first place." He smiled smugly.

"You've got it all figured out," she said. "What have I ever done to you that you would want to ruin my reputation?"

He snarled at her, half laugh, half grimace. His pupils were tiny dots and she wondered what drug he was abusing.

"Nothing," he said. "I always liked you, Mrs. West. But now, you're just convenient. I need money for my plans and you're going to help me get them."

Abruptly, he threw open the door.

"I'll be watching you, so don't get clever and call the cops on me. I know where you live. I know where your daughter and her precious family lives. And," he paused dramatically, "I have pictures."

"Pictures? Of what?"

"You and me at the Me-Too march," he smirked. "You tripped on the curb and fell into my arms. Great shot of you holding me. And I was only seventeen at the time." His eyes lit up with diabolical glee.

"Why do you hate me so much?" she demanded.

He stepped through the door.

"I don't hate you," he said. With a dismissive nod, he blew out of the room.

Juliet let out a deep breath. She could handle this.

She rushed out of the room, looking for security and feeling faint. She needed air, pushed open the nearest exit door, and stood outside gulping deep breaths of the hot, summer night. She had no idea Charles was such a sociopath. He had seemed okay in class although she had sensed a complex energy behind his smiling façade and his need for extra help with assignments. She remembered him fondly when he was ten years old. How he had changed.

Fear rose up in her throat. She spit swiftly behind a rhododendron bush. She choked again and stood holding the wall with her hand. Sweat stood out on her forehead. She didn't like being threatened. It made her hair stand up on end and her blood pressure rise.

A man's voice behind her said, "Are you all right?"

"Go away!" she whirled around, hands up in a fist. She stood staring at her golden pirate, who returned the look of mutual shock.

"Dang, Juliet, what happened to you? Are you sick?" he put a cool hand against her boiling brow. "What happened to you? Should I call the paramedics?"

"No, no, I'm fine, really I am, I'm sorry, I don't know what came over me," she babbled at him. "I was starting to leave and I felt faint and then things got woozy—"

She felt his hands on her brow and arms again.

"You're burning up, come on, you need to go home." He took her knapsack and her arm and started leading her to the parking lot.

"Where are you parked?"

She pointed and he led her to her car. She followed submissively, not daring herself to speak. She wanted to cry with anger.

At the car, he stopped. "Do you have the keys, Juliet?" he asked softly, as to a frightened child.

She fumbled in her bag and found the keys. He took them from her.

"Get in and I'll drive you home," he said.

"No, I'm fine," she said. "I can make it alone."

"Get in, I'll drive you home."

"Do I look that terrible?" she asked angrily.

"Yes," he said, "you look like hell. Scared, too."

"I don't scare easily," she said, "but I had a surprise."

"I know," he said, "so get in."

"What will you do with your car?" she asked him.

"I'll get one of my kids to drive me back here later," he said, pushing her gently in on the seat. He walked around to the driver's side.

"Aren't you afraid someone will steal it?" she asked. "It's awfully isolated around here at night."

"I'm not afraid for a car," he said and looked her straight in the face. She dropped her eyes. He started the engine and drove slowly away from the school. "Do you want to tell me about it?"

"About what?" She took out her handkerchief and water bottle and started cooling off her face and neck.

He looked her up and down. "About what happened. I went to the convenience store to buy a Coke. As I was walking back, I saw the kid running away, running like he was on fire. He got to the edge of the parking lot and then another kid in a black Jeep pulled up and they got away, real fast."

He looked at her sitting there with her eyes closed and blew his stack. "Come on Juliet, what happened? Your clothes don't look funny so you weren't raped or mugged, at least I don't think you were."

"Of course not!" she said indignantly. "Do you think I'm so naive?"

"You sit around in that empty building for hours, with no one around, yeah, I think you're a little naive. Were you robbed?"

She took a tissue out of her purse. "No, I wasn't robbed. I was just surprised by a former student, that's all. I didn't expect to see him, and he upset me. It reminded me of the past, seeing him."

They had stopped at a red light, and she saw him staring at her intently, trying to figure her out.

"All right, I can buy that," he said. "But to puke in the bushes? That must have been quite a past."

"I didn't puke, I spit! And who are you to question my past?" she shouted at him. "We all have struggles and sadness and memories to work through. You should know that after being a Marine."

"I know memories," he said. "Memories that cloud your brain and make your eyes go funny until you go out and build a house or drink a hundred beers and dance real fast in a bar until you get dizzy and the memories go away for a while." He looked at her with sorrow. "I know sadness, too, Juliet, when my wife died, I wished I had been killed and not been sent home with a medal. I wished I was in a wooden box with a flag draped over my heart."

"I'm glad you weren't," she said, with a little shuddering breath. "I am so happy you're here with me."

He let out a sigh. "I hoped you would feel that way," he whispered.

She leaned way back and shut her eyes. They drove in silence until the growling of a stomach made her eyes fly open.

"Was that you or me?" she asked.

"I didn't eat all day," he said. "I worked for a few hours, slept for a few hours, took a shower and ran over here tonight."

"What a serious student you are," she said lightly.

"I couldn't miss my favorite class," he said.

"Your only class," she reminded him.

"And my favorite," he corrected her. "So, I'm hungry."

"Me, too," she said. "I didn't eat much today. I went to the studio this morning and was reading papers this afternoon. I was too restless to eat."

"Then, let's get something," he said and pulled into an all-night restaurant.

He helped her out of the car and very tenderly tucked her arm through his. She felt a thrill of pleasure at his protection, a feeling she hadn't felt in years. He escorted her to a comfortable booth.

She saw the waitress checking him out. Yes, he made a gorgeous escort. She hoped she didn't look like the wrath after her scare and choking and weeping over the rhododendron bushes.

"Juliet?" He handed her a menu and she flipped it open.

"I'll have French toast and coffee," she said.

"And I'll have three fried eggs, bacon, hash browns, pancakes and milk," he said. "Please," he smiled at the waitress and she giggled. What an effect he had on the female of the species.

"Okay?" he watched her drink coffee and sat back to relax.

"Okay," she smiled at last. "I'm sorry I snapped at you."

"No problem," he said, "I know you had a fright. You know what you need?" he took a big swig from his glass of milk. "You need a rub-down, you know, a massage, with soft music and a cool sheet over you. Nice music and candles everywhere and just a tiny bit of French champagne. Then you could relax and get over your scare."

He smiled innocently and yet, there was that air of intense sexuality. She felt like she was sitting in a love brewery. You could bottle and sell him; he was that potent.

"Did you learn all that stuff about massages from your... ah... dancers?" she inquired with round eyes over her coffee cup.

His eyes surveyed her, equally round and innocent.

"No, I taught them a thing or two," he said. "I'm very good with my hands."

Juliet looked at his strong, tanned hands and started to choke on her coffee.

He jumped up and slid into the booth beside her. "Hey, watch it, Mrs. Juliet," he said, and pounded her on the back a couple of times. She felt the warmth of his hand against her shirt and felt his firm leg pressing against hers. His closeness did nothing to calm her down and she sputtered and started to hiccup.

"I'm all right," she gasped and brushed his hand away. "I'm— I'm fine," she said, and coughed and hiccupped again, much to her chagrin.

He kept patting her on the back, but softly now.

"No, please," now she was laughing, really, this was too absurd, she felt like her granddaughter. "I'm fine, go back to your seat, I'll drink some water, I'm fine." She was babbling again and she knew it. Damn, couldn't she get a grip on herself tonight? She took a cautious sip of water and felt a tiny burp erupt through her lips. She giggled and put the glass down with a bang.

"Sorry," she said. "I don't know what came over me. I'm all jangly tonight. I feel like a five-year-old." She hiccupped one last time and clapped a hand over her mouth.

"Do you want me to scare you?" he asked her, watching her with a little smile tugging at his mouth. "That's supposed to cure the hiccups."

"I think I've been scared enough, tonight," she said. "First by Charles and then by you."

The waitress came with their food and after pouring more coffee for Juliet and producing hot sauce for James, went away with another look aimed directly at him. They ate in silence for a minute. Companionable silence, the lovely kind where you don't need to talk to fill in every gap.

"Ah, this is good," he said cutting into a sausage. "Real food." He looked at her. "Is that the kid that jumped you tonight? Charles?"

"I wasn't jumped," she said indignantly. "He just took me by surprise, that's all."

He studied her over his glass of milk. "Are you sure that's all he took?"

"What do you mean?" she asked, her face flushing a bit from the memory of falling in the dark, when she wasn't sure what was happening.

"He didn't try to take anything from you or threaten you in any way?" He was waiting for an answer. She knew her reply had better be good.

"Just information, that's all he wanted," she said at last.

"What kind of information?"

"He was looking for a teacher he used to know, one who used to be a friend of mine," she lied. "That's all."

He ate half a pancake and then studied her face.

"And did you tell him where this friend went?" he asked her.

"No, I mean, I couldn't, because this person passed away last year." she said defensively, seeing his look of disbelief. "Don't you believe me?"

"No, I think you're lying. I think he's got some hold over you."

"He does *not* have a hold over me," she said through clenched teeth.

"It's about that missing book, I bet," he raised his eyebrows at her.

She attempted to stare him down. "You've got it all wrong," she said.

"Okay, if that's the way you want it," he said easily. "Just don't keep getting mugged at night in the dark, in the bushes, when you're all alone, Juliet. I won't always be around to help you."

"I didn't ask you for any help," she said, feeling anger. "You insisted."

"Yeah, I'm real pushy," he said and cut into one of his eggs. "When a man loves a woman, he wants to make sure she stays alive."

"Stop saying that!" she said and smacked her hand on the table. "You can't love me; you've only seen me three times."

"But who's counting?" he grinned at her. She blushed. "Romeo fell in love with Juliet in about five minutes," he said to her with a warm look. "Remember?"

"That was fiction," she said, feeling absurdly upset.

"Was it?" he said with a shrug. "If you say so, Miss teacher lady. I'm too tired to fight with you."

"I don't believe that," she said huffily. "You always look like you're ready to fight."

She got a wink in reply as he drank more milk.

"Relationships are like these eggs, Juliet, did you know that?" he asked her with a wicked grin when he came up for air. She longed to wipe a speck of milk off his budding mustache.

Instead, she looked amused at his abrupt change of subject. "How so?" she asked. "You crack an egg and take your chances?"

"In a way," he said. "But I was thinking that women are like these eggs right here," he pointed to the three on his plate.

"Those eggs don't look like women," she said, sipping coffee and watching him.

"This is a metaphor," he said importantly and smiled like a seventh grader.

"Very, very good, Mr. Sanders," she laughed, and nodded in approval. "You've learned a mountain of knowledge in only two classes."

"I'm good, ain't I?" he beamed, and patted his own broad shoulder. "There's hope for everybody, Mrs. Juliet. But back to these eggs," he said.

"I'm all attention," she said.

"Now this egg here is all hard and the yolk is very firm and you know that when you cut into it, it's gonna be no trouble at all, just all business. Some women are like that," he said. "They're very prim and proper and know exactly what they want from a man and exactly how much they need to give in return to keep the relationship alive. They give only what's expected. No more, no less."

"That sounds pretty cold," she said. "Anyone you know?"

"The first woman I got serious with after my wife passed away was just like that. She had no emotions, she had gotten rid of those a long time ago. It was what can you do for me, Jimmy, and how fast?"

"That sounds pretty bitter," Juliet said. He looked so hurt and unsmiling. He quickly ate up the egg with a frown.

"Well, when you try and romance a woman and every time she lets you kiss her she wants you to fix a leaky faucet or go to the Home Center and buy her some lumber or a new toilet, then you do feel used," he said. "I mean I don't mind being a sex object for a young lady's lust, but if she sees me as just one big tool belt—"

"I see what you mean," Juliet said, fascinated by the image of him stark naked, in cowboy boots, wearing a tool belt with hammers and pliers that hung down like fig leaves.

Quit it, she told herself, *you're getting goofy again.* She pinched her arm above the elbow.

"Why do you do that?" he asked her.

"Do what?"

"Keep pinching yourself like that," he said with a puzzled look. "You do it in class all the time."

"Don't you miss anything?" she said, running her hands through her hair in exasperation.

"I try not to," he said seriously, "especially when the person is so interesting to me. And when I'm falling in love with her."

She was not going there.

"Tell me more about the eggs," she said, "which, by the way are getting cold. How are the rest of those glutinous messes like relationships?"

He laughed, showing off strong white teeth. The pirate Romeo.

"All right, um, this egg here," he pointed to a broken yolk oozing yellow across his plate, "is very clingy, very messy and gooey. It's a very intense love affair, but the woman can't control her emotions and lets it leak all over the place and it makes a mess. I hate that kind of relationship," he said, "you know when you can't even go out for a pack of cigarettes and they're in the window waiting for you all nervous and upset."

"Anyone else you know?" she asked lightly.

"My wife was like that in the early days of our marriage," he said, "she was so worried that I would get hurt on the job or when I was out with the guys that it put a strain on our marriage. And then we had twins and it was like five hundred times more stress for her."

"It's hard being a wife and mother," Juliet said seriously. "There is so much to worry about."

"I know that now," he said. "I was pretty immature when I got married, I was only twenty-one and right out of the service. I hadn't raised enough hell, I guess. I wanted to show her I was the boss, so I would go out and not say where I was going." He laughed a little in disgust. "God, I was a baby, I don't how she stood me. But I did mellow out after a while, so—"

"So, it all worked out," Juliet said.

"Yeah, we were pretty happy. She could have done better, but I couldn't have," he said, looking down at his plate.

Juliet felt a pang of remorse. He was sweet and it was her turn to comfort him now. She reached over and touched his hand.

"I'm sorry," she said, "about your wife. How sad for you to be left alone so young."

"Thank you for understanding," he said and raised her hand to his lips.

She felt the shock of his contact and she felt her insides growing warm with desire. He was nice and so handsome... Would a fling be so bad? After all, it had been such a long time. *And he said he loved her.* Even if it wasn't true, it was nice to hear. She gently tugged her hand away.

"Eat your last egg," she said softly.

"No, I'm full," he said. They both looked at the remaining egg, a perfectly cooked oval, shiny white, with a promise of rich yellow beneath. "This egg is like you, Juliet," he said with a little smile.

"I shouldn't ask," she said, "but go ahead and tell me."

"This egg is perfect. Firm yet tender, not burned or brittle around the edges, a romantic who believes in the power of beauty and in helping others." He prodded the yolk a little with his fork but it would not break. "Tough, too, but in a good way. It takes a lot to upset a strong woman and that's good for a rough guy like me. I like a partner who knows her own mind and who will stick by me."

Juliet stared at him in awe.

"You get an awful lot of insight out of looking at three eggs," she said. "You should go into the fortune-telling business."

"Eggs instead of tea leaves?" He signaled for the check. "That's an idea for me when I retire. I'll start a poultry farm and run a gypsy fortune business on the side."

She held a hand up to her head. She was feeling tired.

"I talk too much," he said and stood up. He held out his hand and gently pulled her to her feet. He was so much taller and once again she felt that wave of relief come over her. His presence was so comforting and so relaxing. She wanted to sleep.

"Here you've been working late in this heat and I'm running on about eggs and women," he said. He paid the bill and they walked outside into the hot, still night. He opened the car door for her. "Why didn't you tell me to shut up?"

"You were so interesting," she said. "I was fascinated."

"That's something, anyway," he said. She put her head back on the seat and closed her eyes for a few seconds. It felt wonderful.

"Juliet," he said softly.

"Yes?" she said, eyes shut, breathing deeply, feeling her stomach and chest relaxing at last.

"Promise me you won't let this thing get out of hand," he said.

"What thing?" she sighed.

"This Charles stalker thing or whatever you want to call it. If anything else happens like tonight, promise me you'll call the police."

"The cops?" she asked with a smile, eyes still shut.

"Yeah, the cops. I've got a couple of very good friends on the force, we could go talk to them."

"So, do I," she said. "One is a retired lieutenant," she said. "I can get plenty of free advice."

"Not advice, Juliet," he put his hand over hers and her eyes flew open at his touch. "But help and protection. Don't let this get out of hand. I don't want you to get hurt."

"All right, I promise. But it's okay, I assure you. One kid asking questions, that's all. He doesn't know anything and I'm not going to tell him anything. We're at a standstill, a freeze-frame, nothing is going to happen." They pulled up in front of her house. "Thank you, for driving me home. Will you call one of your sons now?"

He frowned. "I want to walk you up to the door," he said in a low voice.

"I'm fine," she protested, but her insides were churning.

"Hush, little girl," he said. "I'm going to make sure you're all right."

She felt a warmth suffuse her body. Little girl? A fifty-five-year-old little girl?

"I'll pull around the back and park in your garage," he said and drove around the block. "And see you safely to your door." The alley was quiet, the darkness punctuated by streetlights and by the occasional light from a deck and back porch. The sound of crickets chirping broke the stillness. All was serene until they pulled up in front of her garage door.

There was a word written in red paint on the door. For a moment, she thought it was blood and pinched herself above the elbow again hard. And then again.

CHAPTER SIX

"WHAT THE HELL?" JIM SAID. HE TURNED ON THE FLASHLIGHT ON his phone and jumped out. "You stay here," he ordered and locked the car.

She watched him go up to the garage. He shone the light on the automatic door and up on her deck. No one was in sight, so why was she sitting here like a scared rabbit? Just because a man told her to? She pushed open the door.

"What does it say?" she asked. He was poking around the black garbage dumpster that stood outside her gate.

"You tell me," he said, and flashed the light on the door.

Tall red letters were painted on her white garage door.

"BEWARE," she read in a hoarse voice.

"Beware, what? That's the question" he said, and started tapping the keypad quickly.

"What are you doing?"

"I don't like this, Juliet," he said. "I don't like this at all. We're going to call the cops."

"No, don't. I don't want this incident to blow up into something big," she said, and put a hand on his arm. "Trust me,

James, this is nothing, just a little statement, that's all. Because I wasn't scared tonight."

He looked at her. "I don't know—"

"Trust me, please, it's all right," she said with a confidence she did not feel.

"I don't know," he repeated, staring at the door. He put a finger up to one of the letters. "This smells like oil paint, we'd better get it off quick. Have you got turpentine or paint thinner?"

"In the garage," she said.

"What's going on?" said a voice from across the alley.

"Just a little mess, Lois," she called to her friend.

Lois walked up to them.

"Wow, what a mess. Student of yours?" she asked, without beating around the bush.

"Yes," Juliet admitted. "I had a run-in with one tonight at school. He was looking for something."

"Juliet has been a great mentor to a lot of these kids," Lois explained to Jim. She stuck out her hand, "I'm Lois, a good friend of Juliet's for many years."

"Jim Sanders," he said, "nice to meet you. I'm a student of Juliet's."

Lois looked him up and down and Juliet could feel her intense interest in the handsome man.

"What fun," she said and smiled. "So, kiddo," she turned to Juliet, "are you going to make a report? This is totally illegal, you know."

"No, I'm not," she said. "I don't want to have to talk about it, not right now. Let this ride a bit."

"I hope you know what you're doing," Lois said. "You know you should report this. The patrol cars will come down the alley more at night."

"I know," Juliet said. "But I'm hoping this is just a one-time thing." She saw Jim and Lois watching her carefully in the dim light. "Okay? We're not going to have a fit over some red paint, right?"

"Show me where the turpentine is stored," Jim said, "I want to clean this off."

"I'll make some coffee for you," Lois said, after they found the cleaner in the garage. "Come on, Juliet, let's go inside."

They walked inside; Juliet turned on all the lights. Soon, the smell of fresh dark roast coffee filled the house.

"Only one cup, please," Juliet said, falling into a chair wearily. "Or I won't sleep at all tonight. I just drank three cups."

"With Jim?" Lois stood at the kitchen sink, washing a dish, pouring a glass of water. Always busy, always on the lookout for something to do that would help her friend.

"Yes, he took me out for breakfast," Juliet said with a dreamy look on her face.

"At ten o'clock at night?" Lois giggled. "Okay, Jule, whatever you say. I won't ask what time you two are going to eat dinner. *If music be the food of love* or if food be the music of love or—"

"Please," Juliet put a hand up to her head. "Don't you start mixing metaphors and quoting poetry at me. I've had enough tonight."

"Are you sure you're okay?" Lois asked.

"I'm fine. Tired and a bit confused, but I'm okay."

"Juliet?" a deep voice asked from outside.

"Yes?" Juliet jumped up and walked out on the deck.

"I'm going to use the hose to rinse off the door and the alley, all right?" Jim asked.

"Fine, thank you," she said, staring at his tall body and the enormous shadow he cast over the yard. "Did it come off?"

"Yeah, most of it came off, I'll give it another scrub in the morning, when it's light."

"Thank you, Jimmy," she said softly.

"Hey, I like it when you call me Jimmy, my mom used to call me that," he said, looking straight up at her. In the lamplight he looked larger than life, a pirate Romeo—*Stop it, Juliet, you're getting goofy again.*

"She did?" Juliet kept looking down at him. *Oh speak again, bright angel,* her mind kept repeating. He was so pure and golden, so desirable. She pinched her arm.

"Yeah, she did," he whispered back up to her. "You remind me of her, she was tall and pretty, and so sweet."

Lois coughed behind her. "Everything under control? Out damned spot?"

"My goodness, not more Shakespeare," Juliet groaned. "Fine, Lady Lois Macbeth, most of it's gone," she said.

"Great, well, if you two don't need me anymore, I'm going to go home, I'm waiting for a call and I don't want to miss it."

"Bob?" Juliet asked her.

"Yes, he's in New York on business and ooh, I love to talk to that man," she cooed, and walked slowly down the back stairs. She looked up at Juliet. "Behave yourself, you hear? Or at least," she said with a wink at Jim, "don't do anything I wouldn't, Juliet. Jim, great to meet you."

"Likewise," he said.

"Juliet, I'll check on you in the morning," Lois said, and went home.

"I'm sure you will," Juliet whispered, and walked back into the house to answer her ringing phone.

"Hello?" She fought down a yawn.

"Mom?"

"Colette? Are you all right, honey?" she anxiously asked her daughter. She looked at the clock over the piano. It was five in the morning in London.

"We're fine, Mom, I couldn't sleep and I thought I'd call you. I know sometimes you're up late reading papers and writing, so I didn't think I'd disturb you."

"Oh, sweetheart, you could never disturb me," Juliet said. "Are you having a good time?"

"It's so beautiful and we're all relaxing and enjoying the scenery. Even Angelica is finding plenty to do here. There are so many parks for children to play in."

"I'm glad. And how's Paul?"

A pause. "He's fine. A little worried because…"

"What is it? What's the matter?"

A small sigh but one of happiness. "I'm late, ten days late."

"Oh, honey, that's wonderful!" Juliet was thrilled. Another grandchild, another sweet bundle of joy for her to love and spoil.

"I know, we are so happy," her daughter said. "I bought a home pregnancy test but I wasn't sure if I did it right, so I did a second one. It's positive. I wanted you to be the first, I mean the second to know."

"Thank you, sweetie," Juliet said. "I'm so happy for all three of you. Be careful until you get home."

"That's what Paul thinks," her daughter said. "He thinks we should come home early and go to my regular doctor instead of doing the week in Paris, but I told him, it will be years before we come back and I am not going to miss eating real brie cheese!"

"Heaven forbid," Juliet said. "And don't forget the camembert and the roquefort."

"Ooh I can't wait," Colette sighed. "And all that lovely pâté de foie gras, fresh croissants and brioche."

"Enjoy the scenery, the food, and the romance of Paris," Juliet said with a sigh. She had always wanted to go to Paris with a lover.

"We will enjoy Paris," her daughter said. "I will remember this trip always."

"Juliet?" Jim said behind her.

"Who's that, Mother?"

"Um, nobody."

"Juliet, I'm going to put your car away and lock up the garage."

"Thank you, Jim, uh, thanks, that's great," she stammered.

He left the house and she could hear her car being moved into the garage.

"Who's Jim?" her daughter demanded from four thousand miles away.

"Just a student of mine, who helped me tonight."

"What happened?" Colette asked.

"Just a flat tire, that's all," Juliet said. "And he helped me to get home," she explained.

"It's eleven o'clock, Mother," Colette said.

"Yes, dear, I know," Juliet laughed. "I get your point."

"Is he safe? Can you trust him?"

Juliet paused and thought. *Could she trust him?*

"Mother?"

"I'm so happy for you, dear," Juliet said, "give Paul and the baby a big kiss for me."

"How old is this student, Mother?"

"Old enough," Juliet said. "Love you, dear."

"Juliet?" She heard his voice from the back yard.

She walked out on the deck. "I'm here."

"Was that your daughter?" Jim said.

"Yes, she's in London on a vacation with her husband and my granddaughter. She thinks she's pregnant and she wanted to call me. She couldn't sleep."

He leaned against the wall and yawned.

"You two must be very close."

"We are, very close. I miss her so."

"When is she coming back?" he yawned again, and she joined in with him.

"In two weeks, they are going to Paris before they come home. Her husband is worried about her because she's going to have a baby. But Colette is strong, travel won't bother her. She'll be home before she gets even a minute of morning sickness."

"That's great," Jim yawned again. "I'm sorry, Juliet, but I'm ready to keel over. Do you want me to sleep here on the couch or do you have a guest room for me?"

CHAPTER SEVEN

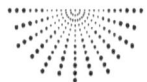

He walked up the back steps.

"What?" she asked him. Her mind felt numb. "Sleep here?"

"Yeah, I think I should sleep here. I don't want anything to happen to you tonight."

"Nothing is going to happen." She looked at him in protest and walked over to where he leaned against the deck wall. "Really, nothing will, I promise."

"It's not up to you, babe," he said, and lightly flicked her nose. "It's up to the powers that be, ain't it? They might want to come back one more time, to see the pretty Miss teacher lady. No, I'm going to be right here in case there's trouble. I told Lois I would look after you."

"Oh, you did, did you?" she asked faintly, feeling outmaneuvered, and vulnerable.

"Yeah, I did, and a Marine never goes back on his word."

"I'm a big girl," she said, "I can look after myself."

"Can you? Can I see the rest of your house? Let me check to see if the windows are locked. You can put on your AC to stay cool tonight."

She extended a hand. "Go ahead," she sighed. She followed

him as he checked the kitchen, living room, small sewing room, and bathroom. He locked the door which led to the basement.

He walked into her daughter's old bedroom. It was still decorated in her favorite shades of lilac and ivory. "Pretty room, but not for me," he said. "All those sweet dolls on the bed would make me nervous."

"I'm sure they would," she said. "You don't look like the type to play with dolls."

"Only live dolls," he said with a wink.

"You're incorrigible," she said. He looked at her oddly.

"That's a good word for me to learn; incur— incur— what?"

"Incorrigible, means shameless and wild."

"I can do wild," he smiled.

"Okay, should I throw you out? Can I physically toss a pirate from my house? Make you walk the plank from my deck?" She giggled and he looked at her, trying to figure out her mood.

"Miss teacher lady, you seem mighty weird, right now. I think you need to sleep."

"I will sleep, as soon as you leave," she said firmly. He walked past her into her daughter's bedroom and returned carrying a mound of lilac-colored blankets and pillows.

"Right," he said. "Excuse me." He gently elbowed past her and started laying blankets and sheets down on the huge ivory leather sofa her ex-husband had won in a poker game eleven years ago.

"What are you doing?" she demanded.

"What does it look like, Juliet?" he said. "I'm sleeping right here on this funky, leather couch you got, so if any trouble shows up in the middle of the night, I'll be here to help you."

"My hero," she said with a scowl.

"Don't be a witch, right now, okay?" he pleaded. "I know you're exhausted, God knows, I'm about ready to fall down with my hangover and chasing you around parking lots and eating eggs and washing garage doors, so if you could please just shut up for a little while, Miss lovely lady, and let me sleep here until I got enough strength to go home…"

"You don't have a car!" she said in shock. "You left it at school."

"Right," he whipped out his cell phone and dialed rapidly.

"Yeah, Mike? Dad here, my car is at the Thomas Jefferson College. In the lot. Go there tomorrow morning early and bring it over to—" he paused, "What's the address again, Juliet?"

"4140 N. Magnolia," she said faintly. She couldn't believe he was sleeping here.

"4140 N. Magnolia," he repeated. "Mind your mouth," he said to his son. "I'm helping a teacher and I want you to be respectful. Okay. How's your brother? All right." He smiled at her.

"What must they be thinking?" she asked him. "Or are they used to Papa sleeping out and needing his car rescued?"

"I told you, don't get bitchy, it's too late and you're way too pretty for that," he said, and dove into the mound of blankets he had prepared. He sat up for a minute, tore off his boots and without a word pulled off his t-shirt and lay down again.

Juliet was mesmerized by his long, hard muscular torso lying on her couch. In truth, he was gorgeous, a perfect Adonis, a modern Hercules. She stared at him in fascination, because he was so buffed, tanned and muscled. He watched her studying him.

"Do I pass?" he asked her.

"Excuse me?" she asked him.

"Do I pass? How do I look? What kind of grade would you give me for strength?" he asked her innocently. "You know, if you was a judge and I was the one in a bodybuilding competition?"

"Oh, I'd give you an A plus," she sighed, and walked into the bathroom. The sound of his laughter burned her ears as she firmly shut the door and turned the lock.

She took a quick, hot shower. Her muscles were stiff from the tension and the fall in the dark classroom. She watched the water flood over her tall, voluptuous body that had both curves and muscles. She enjoyed being touched and she enjoyed touching. But she was going to make a straight beeline for her room. She would not look at the hunk on her sofa. She would be good. If she fell into his trap, she would be stuck forever.

Juliet quickly dried off and put on her chaste pink and white flowered cotton nightgown with the matching lace-trimmed robe. A real grandmother's gown, her family had given it to her for last Mother's Day. She put on pink satin slippers and recklessly added a spritz of perfume. She ran a comb through her hair and massaged her aching fingers with hand cream. *No use scaring the man,* she thought.

She tiptoed out of the bathroom. The lights were off in the living room and she thought he must have dropped off to sleep. Just as she put her hand on the bedroom door she heard him say, "Hey, Juliet, you got any whiskey? I could use a little nightcap."

"I thought you were sleeping," she said, walking up carefully to the sofa.

"No, I'm just laying here thinking," he said. "Got any?"

"Yes, of course," she walked over to an antique dry sink which had been turned into a liquor cabinet. "I think we have some Jack Daniel's here," she said, poking through bottles underneath. "My ex drank whiskey."

"Thank God for that," Jim sighed and took the shot glass she handed him. "Aren't you going to join me?"

"I never drink whiskey anymore," she said. "Except when I'm getting a cold."

He got up and poured her a tiny glass.

"Here, take a little sip, it's medicinal, good for treating shock."

"I'm not in shock," she said, and sat down on the edge of the sofa.

"Yes, you are," he said. "First, having me in your class was a real shock. I'm a smart-ass and you don't need that after a long day of trying to teach. And then you're in the middle of Act One, Scene Two with a punk writing weird junk on your castle door.

It's enough for a nice lady like you." He lay on the sofa with his feet inches away from her. She took a tiny sip and coughed.

"Wow, this is brutal stuff," she said, laughing. "I'm out of practice."

"I know you are," he said, watching her in the dim light cast from the nightlight in the kitchen. "But it's okay, Juliet, I'm going to help you. I could teach you a few things."

"Like what?" she said, instantly tensing up. "More poetry?"

He sat up and moved closer to her.

"*She jests at scars that never felt a wound*," he said softly. "Don't make fun of me, Juliet. Please, don't. You see, I haven't fallen in love with a woman in twenty years and I forget how to be sweet and what to say and how not to scare her away. I'm such a rough dude."

She turned her head and stared at him.

"You keep talking about love," she said. "Don't you mean infatuation? The big rough Marine falling in love with the schoolteacher. Poetry is so appealing and seductive," she said, "especially when you're not used to it."

"You're appealing and seductive," he said and started to massage her neck and shoulders.

She squeezed her glass tightly in her fingers as she felt his warm hands on her tired, tense skin, and sighed.

"Breathe," he ordered. "Take a deep breath in and let it out." He took the glass out of her hands and put it down. He turned her face towards him. "Breathe, Juliet. You've taken on so much for so many. You need to rest, honey." His voice was low and soft like molten honey, oozing over her tired nerves and frazzled senses. His hands kept up a gentle roving motion over her shoulders and neck. She tilted her head to one side and closed her eyes. It felt good, he felt good, she was relaxed with this giant Romeo who said he loved her and was probably just talking beautiful nonsense that he had read in one of the books he carried in the back pocket of his tight jeans. Did she have to know everything about him just to be close to him? Was it so bad to feel this good?

He lowered his head to hers and she instinctively opened her eyes. "Juliet," he said, "let me kiss you, baby." His warm mouth covered her trembling lips. She was immediately transported above space and time to a warm, protective cocoon of sensuality. She no longer was in her own Victorian house, with the leaky attic and the noisy plumbing, but in a time warp as real as Verona in 1400. With his lips on hers and his arms around her, gently rubbing her back, she was Shakespeare's Juliet, she was thirteen, and with her Romeo's love she would be new baptized.

She broke away to take a breath.

"Oh, James," she gasped, "we shouldn't be doing this."

"Why not?" he said, and gently lay her down on the couch. "I'm Romeo and you're my Juliet and I want to make love to you."

She stared up at him, eyes wide, unable to move. His tall, lean body poised above her promised immeasurable pleasures. She had no way of knowing but she guessed instinctively that he would be tender and gentle. She felt that she would be able to discover new-found realities about her own sexuality, which had never been completely explored with her ex and had not been able to flower with anyone else since her divorce. She was afraid. She felt fear and apprehension even though she thought she might be about to know the greatest joy of her life. She wanted to open her arms and embrace him and she also wanted to run away. What if he found her old? What if he thought her skin was baggy when they had shed their clothes and lay embraced in the cold light of the moon?

Why didn't she get up and go to bed without him? She had only met this disturbing student two weeks ago and now she was in his arms.

"What are you thinking about?" he was still staring at her with that relaxed, dreamy expression. "Are you still in shock?"

"Yes," she said, "I'm in shock because I'm lying here with you and I'm having all kinds of prurient thoughts about you."

"What does that mean?" he wrinkled his nose and lay down beside her.

"It means I'm having sexy thoughts about you," she admitted.

"Cool. I'll remember that. Are you going to teach me something else tonight, Miss Juliet?"

He nuzzled her shoulder and put his lips against her neck. She trembled with delight and something more intense and primal. *I'm new baptized with his love*, she thought.

"No, I think you are going to do the teaching," she gasped as his mouth trailed burning light kisses down the front of her pink nightgown.

He wrapped himself around her and they kissed at first with the tentativeness of teenagers and then with the full-blown passion of two adults who had just discovered a very precious gift at a more complicated time of life. Debts, children, work and crumbling homes were all forgotten as they explored each other's mouths with an intensity that Juliet had only experienced in dreams. He was tender and yet so strong, she couldn't have moved away unless she had asked him to release her. And she wasn't going to ask.

"Juliet, let me take this off you, I want to see your beauty," he murmured, and gently removed her robe and nightgown. Then he tore off his jeans and briefs and took her into his arms. She lay back again in delight, clad only in pink satin panties and their mingled scent which had permeated her skin. He took a moment to study her as his fingers traced lazy circles along her legs and back.

"You're so beautiful, you're like a proud princess from the middle ages. I can see you taming unicorns and casting magic spells on weary knights and Vikings." He sighed in pleasure. "Who would have thought behind those glasses and those books you were such a hot, mysterious lady?"

"I'm glad you approve," she said, feeling pleasure and warmth from his scrutiny.

"I sure do, I'm in heaven," he said. "I knew something was up when I saw you in class. I thought, she can't be real, she's too gorgeous to be a teacher." Juliet blushed from his praise. "I never thought I could feel this way for a woman again. You have saved my life, Juliet. *With your love I will be new baptized, henceforth I never will be* James Sanders."

"What did you say?" Now she was in shock. Was he reading her mind?

"You know, Romeo said that to his lady."

"Yes, I know, I was just thinking about that a moment ago," she said.

"See? We're on the same wavelength, Juliet, we were meant to be together. It's fate."

She had known love in the past and she had known sorrow, but not what happened during the next hour. He kissed her until she was gasping for breath and their bodies were slick with warmth and passion. He trailed kisses all over her trembling body and when his mouth found her aching bosoms she moaned. He was gentle and tender and never rushed, not even when she touched his manhood and gently rubbed it between her strong hands.

"Oh, God," he had sighed into her skin. He slid off her panties while they exchanged deep kisses and hugs that seemed to capture her soul. Finally, when she was about to beg him to get inside her, he stood up and stretched like a proud, untamed warrior. He was naked, unashamed, beautifully and perfectly male. She reached out to him but he laughed and took her hands.

"I want to make you mine in a real bed, your bed," he said. "Sofas are for kids." He swooped down and scooped her up in his arms. She was tall but she felt tiny and protected in his rock-hard embrace. He slowly walked into her bedroom. A cool breeze blew in from the open windows. The dim light from her nightstand made them seem young and magical. She *was* Juliet when she was in his arms. He *was* her Romeo, and she did believe that he loved her.

He laid her gently down on the bed. The ceiling fan sent soothing puffs of air over their heated skin. She reached up to him.

"James," she whispered.

He was looking down at her tenderly. "Honey, I don't think I can get you pregnant anymore, can I?"

"No, I don't have to worry about that." She hesitated. "I know you've had a lot of girlfriends lately, James, so should we use—"

"I'm okay," he said seriously. "My sons make me have a test every January, like a Happy New Year's present, Dad, you're still alive and well, but this year, I haven't been with anyone at all. I've been waiting for someone like you, Juliet. Someone wonderful."

She reached up again for him. "Come here," she whispered.

"Love, I'm here," he said and immediately lay down gently on top of her. He entered her with a swiftness and total possession that left her gasping for breath. He started a tempo of passion and fulfillment that she had never known before. She grabbed his back with her hands and as they kissed they called each other names of love and total wonder. His thrusts became deeper and more powerful. Juliet held on to him with all her strength and waited for the moment of rapture to take her. When it did arrive, she shuddered and gasped and saw him staring down at her with a face filled with delight.

"Juliet," he smiled. "My lady," he moaned and then his own moment of fulfillment arrived, and they both entered a land that was more enduring than fantasy because it was real and they were together.

CHAPTER EIGHT

JULIET OPENED HER EYES. IT WAS DAWN. SHE WAS IN HER PEACH bedroom with the ivory lace curtains and the Tiffany stained-glass lamp on the nightstand. On her oak dresser stood pictures of her beloved family and a Barbie doll from her granddaughter, to keep her company, so "she wouldn't have to be alone at night."

She was most certainly not alone. She blinked, and in the light saw her companion of the night. He filled the bed magnificently; every raw inch of him was sprawled out upon the cool linen sheets like the lover he had been, like the lover he now was.

My God, Juliet thought. *What have I done?* In one hour I threw away all my good intentions. He stirred a little and she studied his sleeping face. He looked so young, so beautiful, a renegade knight in jeans and boots. His Jeep was his chariot, his cell phone a modern sword. He dueled with his mouth and arms and tongue —oh, God, what had she done?

He opened one eye and in that moment, Juliet fell instantly in love. What did her pirate lover do when he saw the object of his affections in the early light of day? He moved closer, threw his arm about her waist protectively, said, "love you, Juliet," and went back to sleep.

Damn, she thought, did he have to be so cute? He looked twenty-three instead of forty-three and even with his two-day golden stubble on his chin and his spiky golden blond hair all over his head, he was adorable. Last night he had been so sweet.

She lay in bed, drowsily replaying the evening in her mind. The sounds of the birds and the train in the distance were like a symphony. He had played her mind and her body like a fine violin and she had responded to his expertise. What now?

She looked over on the floor. A small book lay there. Always interested she found herself staring at the Penguin Edition of Romeo and Juliet, college bound in pink with the stylized lovers on the cover, reaching across a balcony.

WOW. Had he brought that into her boudoir so he could—as he called it—'lay some lines on her?' Was he really trying to become a real live Romeo? She wickedly leaned over and kissed him below the tiny gold stud in his ear. *His day jewelry*, she thought. Appropriate and tasteful for a student pirate. She nibbled for a moment on a soft earlobe.

"Hey," he said, "cut it out."

"It's morning," she said. "It's time to get up."

"It's not day," he said. *"It was the nightingale, and not the lark, that pierced the fearful hollow of thine ear,"* he said sleepily.

"It was the lark, the herald of the morn, no nightingale," she said, and leaned her body against the length of his firm, warm flesh. How good he felt to her. *"Night's candles are burnt out."*

"That's what I mean," he said and opened his eyes, "couldn't Shakespeare just say, hey it's morning, babe and I gotta go? No, *night's candles are burnt out*, it's so—"

"Poetic?" she asked him with a smile.

"Yeah, poetic," he leaned over and kissed her on the mouth. "And you're poetic. You're gorgeous. How old did you say you were? Does your mother know you're here, little girl? Am I gonna get arrested for taking you to bed last night? Because, dear lady," he kissed her again, "you look around eighteen years old."

"Thank you, sir," she said with a thrill. "You're a liar, but you're so sweet. I know what I can look like in the morning."

"Yeah? Like what?" he challenged her. "I see a young girl with love in her eyes and music in her heart and a body like a gazelle, that's what I see."

She wanted to cry. Why was he so sweet? She didn't want him to go.

"Yon light is not daylight, I know it, I," she said, turning her face to the window. *"It is some meteor that the sun exhales... Stay yet. Thou need'st not to be gone."*

"Is that an invitation, Juliet?" he asked her with a lazy smile. The pupils in his eyes were as wide and black as the deep, dark sea, she noticed before he claimed her lips and body with his own.

They slept after their lovemaking, until a phone somewhere in the house, rang again and again.

"Your landline?" he asked, nuzzling her neck with his lips.

She stroked his face tenderly and listened. "No, wait, that's your phone," she said.

James rolled out of bed and put his feet firmly on the floor. He stretched and yawned and then in three quick steps ran out of her bedroom and grabbed his phone and his clothes. When he walked back to her, he was still naked, unashamed and amused, holding boots and briefs.

"Why are you calling so early?" he asked one of his sons. "Oh, I see, yeah, come by now, I'm ready. Shut your mouth and bring me some of that coffee you're so busy slurping... Right, see ya Mike." He switched off the phone. "That was my son. They're having some problems at the site. Plumbing and sewers issues and the city inspector is there screaming at us. I've got to go."

"Of course, it's a work-day. I understand," she said, sitting up a little and wrapping the sheet around her.

"I don't want to go," he said softly, looking at her. His nakedness revealed his energy and his interest in her.

"You have to go to work. And so do I," she said, pinching herself above the elbow, under the sheet, reminding herself that the dream was over. It was morning and she was back to being herself.

He sighed and picked up the book off the floor. He turned a couple of pages and read to her, *"it is the lark that sings so out of tune, straining harsh discords and unpleasing sharps, some say the lark makes sweet division; this doth not so, for she divideth us,"* he said with a burning look at her. *"O now, begone. More light and light it grows."*

"More light and light, more dark and dark our woes!" she answered him.

"What woes, honey, everything is going to be all right. Don't worry, I'll be back later."

"I didn't mean—"

"What did you mean?" he pulled on his pants and boots and sat down next to her. "Are you worried about that kid last night? I told you, let's go to the cops. Get a protection order, get extra patrols."

"No, I'm not worried about him, I'm not," she assured him, studying the shape of his cheekbones, the curve of his upper lip.

"Are you worried about us?"

"What's us?" she asked him. "We barely know each other."

"For now," he said. "But before this summer's through, we're gonna know each other really well, I promise you that, Juliet." He raised her hand to his lips. *"This bud of love by summer's ripening breath, may prove a beauteous flower when next we meet."*

He smiled at her and her heart lurched. "See, how much I remember? That was the first thing I learned from you."

"And then you laid it on another babe," she said, with a wicked sparkle in her eye.

"Ouch, don't remind me," he grimaced. "I was immature then. I had not gotten to know you. I was not yet baptized." He kissed her hand. "I wasn't in love with you, yet."

She felt a pang. How could he be so sure, so soon? He had finished pulling on his clothes.

"My lady, I've got to go. I'm going to go check on your garage door before my son comes." She started to move. "Don't get up, go back to sleep, it's only seven. Sleep in," he advised. "I'll make some coffee for you before I go." He leaned over and kissed her again. "Sleep. I order you to."

"You're so bossy," she said, and snuggled back into the pillows.

"Yeah, I know," he said. "Always have been." He looked out the window. "Dang. No time to make coffee. There's Mike. I gotta go, babe. *One kiss, and I'll descend.*" He leaned over and kissed her sweetly on the mouth. She felt his warmth and his tenderness and she felt a moment of panic.

"O, think'st thou we shall ever meet again?" Fool, she thought, *stop fishing.*

"I doubt it not, love," he said and winked at her. Then he was gone.

Juliet rolled over and over in her bed. She couldn't fall back to sleep. The sheets and pillows were scented with the smell of James and their night of passion. But after the sheets were washed and the day had come and gone, what would remain?

She got up, took a shower, looked at her emails, and put in a load of wash. She would go to the yoga studio and then come home and write. She didn't have a class today, thank goodness, she knew she was going to crash later in the afternoon. When she went out to the alley to get her car, the garage door was a perfect, pristine white again. There were no signs of the intruder from the night before, no vestiges of red paint remained.

Who would have thought the old man to have so much blood in him? She pinched herself again and got out the car. She was not Lady Macbeth; she was Juliet West. Must she find a quote for everything?

She went to the studio. She stretched luxuriously on her mat, and attended a class, but did not feel as sore as she expected. Maybe later she would feel the beautiful soreness of lovemaking.

Lois eyed her carefully from the next mat.

"You okay?" her friend asked her.

"I'm fine, thanks for asking," Juliet said, and righted herself.

"How's our friend? And where is he? You two looked pretty chummy last night."

"He cleaned my garage door, drank a little whiskey and then left."

"That's all?" Lois looked clearly disappointed.

"That's all," said Juliet firmly. Better start lying now if she was going to protect her professional reputation or maintain this goody-two-shoes type of personality she seemed so intent on having.

"I had hoped—"

"We'll go out again, don't rush us," Juliet said. "I've only known him a week."

"True," Lois said and went over to replace her mat. "I guess you're more sensible than I could be with a hunk like that around."

Sensible? What a laugh, Juliet thought. *I fell for him like straw in the wind.*

When she got home from the studio and the grocery store, there were two messages on her machine. The first was from her daughter, telling her everything was fine and they would call her from Paris. The second was from Jim.

"Hey Miss Juliet, thanks for the best night of my life. I love you, honey and I'll call you later." She felt his warmth suffuse her entire body. My goodness, the effect even his voice had on her. It couldn't be legal.

She worked on a poetry anthology, a collection of poems from women students and faculty, that she was editing, cleaned the kitchen, and tried to take a nap. Finally, she did settle down with some brie cheese, French bread and a glass of pinot grigio.

She would have to rethink her thoughts about her diet; who wanted to be thin anyway? A little treat now and then wouldn't hurt. And after all, she hadn't slept much last night. She needed the fuel for energy.

She kept looking at the phone and then got annoyed with herself.

You're not a teenager, do you want him to call you every five minutes? But last night felt like a dream, *a dream that was too flattering sweet to be substantial*, like Romeo had said. Even grandmothers needed assurance once in a while.

She put on an old movie and when she finally fell asleep Fred Astaire was holding Ginger Rogers in his arms, about to dance the night away.

CHAPTER NINE

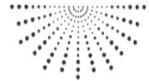

SHE WENT TO SCHOOL THE NEXT DAY IN A WEIRD MOOD. SHE HAD dreamed the entire night of Vikings and pirates and middle-aged Romeos with earrings, cowboy boots and sports t-shirts that said Lions and Tigers and Bears, oh my! and she was about to snap. She had taken her mood enhancing vitamins, she was thinking of taking an anxiety pill, if she didn't calm down. She had two classes on Thursdays and she needed to be bright and intelligent.

Instead, she was feeling very mushy and wanted to go take a nap. This wasn't like her, she usually was full of energy, but after Jim's lovemaking she was in a mood. Not a bad mood, just a mood. She wondered how he would act towards her tonight. She had taken extra care with her appearance. Carefully applied make-up, ankle strap sandals, a form fitting black linen dress that buttoned down the front, and her signature silver jewelry. She had even gone to have her hair touched up this morning and styled. Why was she acting just like a high school girl getting ready for the prom? Or her first date. And this wasn't either.

She got through her first class, held her regular office hours, sipped iced tea and ate a chopped salad in the cafeteria, and met with colleagues about fall classes. Tonight, after class she was going to stop in at a cocktail party for one of the former teachers at the school. It was Jeff and Lydia Hill's fortieth anniversary and they had invited many friends from the college. Forty years. She had made twenty-five, but even that had been an effort. She was wistful, thinking of having a partner to grow old with.

She nervously waited for her evening class to arrive. She chatted with a few students and passed out the night's questions. She waited until 7:02 and then she began. One seat was conspicuously empty in the back of the room. She refused to let that bother her.

By 7:30 she guessed he wasn't coming, by 7:55 she knew it. *My God*, he had blown her off. One night and he didn't have to come to class anymore? Had he gotten what he had wanted? She was furious, she felt the psychic anger going down to her polished toes but she finished the class with her usual grace and packed up to go to the party.

The nerve. No call, no note, no nothing. She was so disturbed that she didn't even recall the more ominous events of the other night, when she had been shoved into a classroom against her will. That seemed like a year ago to her.

Quit acting so huffy, Juliet. It's only one class, he probably had to work. You are acting like a babe in the woods, again. This is what love did to people, made them crazy. That was one of the reasons that she had not wanted to fall into bed with practically a complete stranger. You never knew what they were really like.

She drove the five minutes to the party having a conversation with him in her mind. She was giving him a piece of her mind and she was doing it beautifully. *Just you wait, Henry Higgins*, she thought, singing the song from My Fair Lady in her head. *I'm going to give you the brush off, if I ever see you again.* The party was in a condo overlooking Lake Shore Drive and when Juliet gave her car to the valet to park, she wondered how many people like herself would be there alone. She was used to it by now, not having a partner or a date but it seemed there were more and more couples lately at these functions. She was one of the singles, the solo satellites circling the party looking for a connection.

But was she looking? She had gotten used to her dignified solitary life… or she thought she had. My God, in one week, she had thrown all good sense and caution to the wind. *And she missed him.*

The party was in full swing and she saw many friends from work. A waiter passed out champagne and cucumber sandwiches on a silver tray. Caviar and icy vodka was being passed around by another white-gloved attendant. Her hosts had spared no expense to celebrate. Their lovely immense apartment was filled with African and Chinese artwork and French country furniture. In the corner, a baby grand piano was being played by a professional entertainer. She recognized the tune *"I've got a crush on you, sweetie pie,"* before she recognized the tall man standing with his back to her near the piano. He was talking to the Hills and was very close to a pretty young girl wearing a strapless black dress.

"Juliet," her host said, "my dear, you look wonderful."

She kissed Jeff and his wife Lydia.

"Many, many more happy years," she said, and toasted them with her champagne glass.

"Let me introduce you to a friend of ours," Lydia said. "Jim, this is Juliet West. Jim's son used to be in class with our son, and his company updated this condo for us when we bought it."

He extended a hand to her and she was unable to refuse it. He was wearing a navy blue blazer over new jeans with an ivory linen shirt and his boots were a tasteful black for a change. *Where does he get so many boots,* she wondered, shaking his hand calmly although her pulse was racing out of control.

"I'm so glad to meet you," he said, giving her a warm look that could bubble the vodka right out of his glass.

"How nice," she said coolly.

"This is Veronica," he said, introducing the young woman to her. "She's a friend of the family."

"How do you do?" she said to the girl.

The girl smiled and shook her hand. She was slim and auburn-haired, and her long nails were bright scarlet. Her hands looked like they never washed a dish or did any work. *The nerve,* introducing his date to her. *And friend of what family?* The Addams family? The Montagues? The Capulets? She was ready to run James through with a sword, if only she could find one. He must be having a good laugh at her expense.

At the first possible break in the conversation, she moved away. She would stay another half hour and then go. She moved over to the bar and got a club soda. She stood with her back to him, wishing he would leave.

"Aren't you speaking to me?" said a voice behind her.

She slowly turned around.

"Should I be?"

"Don't be mad at me," he pleaded softly. "I had to take her here tonight. She wants to get into college and her dad is an old friend of mine. He wanted me to introduce her to the Hills. He thought they might be able to help her."

"She needs help?" Juliet asked coolly, watching the girl flirt with a couple of men that were circling her like sharks around a buffet.

Jim smiled. "Academic help," he said. "Her grades aren't that good."

"I see," Juliet said. "She looks like she can hold her own socially."

"Don't be mad at me, Juliet," he said. "Come on out here, I want to talk to you." He grabbed her arm and subtly squeezed it. She held her ground and his eyes widened. "Wanna wrestle?" he asked with a wink. She was aghast.

"How can you be so fresh?" she hissed at him. He winked again. She didn't want to start a scene right here. Against her better judgment she let him guide her out onto the balcony. The stars shone over the dark lake and the warm night air ruffled her hair. She thought of how they had lain together with the night air caressing their bodies and she pinched her elbow. Twice.

He caught her movement.

"Ouch," he grimaced. "Don't be mad at me, Juliet," he repeated. "I didn't want to take her. I thought you'd be here tonight and I was afraid that—"

"That I'd get the wrong idea?"

"How could I explain it? Juliet, I love you, but I gotta take this young babe to a party so she can get into college because she's dumber than a box of rocks."

Juliet laughed in spite of herself.

"That's not very flattering to Veronica," she said. "And you've got a lot of nerve criticizing someone else's brains."

"Ouch, Miss teacher lady, you're right, I'm dumb, too," he said and grabbed her hand. "Forgive me?"

She tugged her hand away and looked resolutely over the balcony.

"For what?"

"For not calling, for being scared to let you know I couldn't go to class tonight."

"You're a big boy, you can play hooky whenever you want," Juliet said lightly and turned to look at him. The light in his eyes almost knocked her off her high-heeled Italian sandals.

"I want to see you later, Juliet, please let me come by."

"Tonight?" she said. "It's so late. And besides," she looked back at the young lady who was laughing into her champagne, "you've got a date."

"She's not a date," he said seriously. "She's work. She's as bad as a stopped-up sewer or a house full of termites. She needs a lot of TLC."

"Your metaphors are getting better every day," Juliet told him coolly. "No, I'm going home in a little while, alone."

"Come on, don't be mad, I've thought about you day and night. I keep getting weak in the knees whenever I remember how well you fit in my arms, under my body—"

"Hush!" Juliet looked over her shoulder. "Not here." She also felt weak in the knees. She was about ready to keel over with his nearness and the memory of their evening and morning together. "This is not the place."

"Then, I'll come by your house. I'll be there in an hour."

"It's almost ten now," Juliet said. "Don't you ever have to get up and work in the morning?"

"All the time," he said. "But when I got something important to do, I do it. And lady, you're important to me."

Juliet looked at him and let out a breath. The pirate Romeo, looking just a little unsure of himself. His gold earring glimmered in the light, his eyes shone with desire and tenderness.

"All right," she said, unable to stop herself. "I'll be home later."

"I'll be over," he said, "as soon as I return that young lady to the nursery. Or the nunnery, like your Bard says."

"She hardly looks like a nun," Juliet said, watching the girl throw back her head and laugh recklessly. He grabbed her hand and gave it a quick kiss.

"You never know," he said, "she might be holier than she looks. *Thinks't thou?*"

He was gone and she was smiling.

She went and talked to some more people she knew and sat down by the piano for a while. She loved cocktail piano, she knew all the old torch songs. In fact, the torchier the song, the better she liked it. The tunes were so romantic.

You'd be so easy to love… sang the piano player and Juliet wondered if James was a good dancer. She was sure he would be, he had such a natural grace and rhythm and moved so well on his feet.

"Are you a good friend of Jim's?" said a voice beside her.

Veronica, slightly rumpled and slightly fried from tossing off too many glasses of champagne, Juliet thought.

"He's a student of mine," Juliet said coolly.

"Really? That's so cool," Veronica said. "I know Mike's in college and Randy keeps going back and dropping out but I didn't know about Jim."

"Are they all good friends of yours?" Juliet asked, trying to remember what it was like to be twenty-one again.

The girl giggled and put a hand up to her cleavage, which was well exposed in the strapless black gown.

"I'll say," she said. Her voice dropped to a whisper. "Don't tell anyone, but I've dated all three of them."

"All three of them?" Juliet repeated.

"Yes, it's a scream, first I went out with Mike and then Randy and then I went out with Jimmy, too."

"You went out with their father?" Juliet watched Jim from across the room laughing and talking with a group of people. He looked so relaxed.

"Yes," she giggled. "Can you believe it? Really, the guys dared me to. So, I did." She looked at Jim and sighed. "He took me to a French restaurant but the food gave me the burps. Garlic and snails. Ugh. I couldn't stop laughing." She sighed again. "I'm too young for him, I guess. He told me he likes more mature women. Like you," the girl said, studying Juliet's face carefully.

Juliet smiled graciously. "I'm sure he enjoyed your company," she said. "You're very charming, Veronica."

"Oh, do you think so? That's nice coming from you, Juliet. My dad says I'm such an airhead."

"I am sure you have a lot of potential, Veronica. Don't always listen to what men tell you."

"That's good advice," the girl said, looking at her with respect. "I do have a mind of my own."

"I am sure you do," Juliet said kindly. "Don't give up on college. It's worth the effort to get a degree."

Juliet saw James looking at her. Swiftly, she stuck out her tongue like a three-year-old. His eyes widened in appreciation and he gave her a thumbs up. She stood and found her hosts to say goodbye. She moved quickly and was gone before he could get away to talk to her.

She drove home slowly, thinking about the evening. So, he liked to take out really young women. Then what was he doing in her bed, talking about love and the eternal connection? *You're just a fling, girlfriend,* she thought. Go home and lock your doors.

She parked her car and quickly looked around the garage. It was bright with light and she shook herself a little. Since the incident with the paint on her garage door, she had been a little ill at ease in the alley. She hated being frightened around her own home. It made her angry.

Everything was quiet. The crickets chirped, a dog barked down the street, and she could hear the ballgame on the radio of her next-door neighbor. She went up the steps to the deck and almost fell over with fright. Sitting at the outdoor dining table was a body!

"What the heck," she said softly, and almost tripped over her feet. The person did not move or speak, he was sitting rigidly in a chair, head slumped over the red-checked tablecloth. There was such an air of unreality to the body that she knew that it was not, could not be real. She walked up and firmly pushed at the intruder invading the privacy of her deck.

The stolen store mannequin was dressed in a black shirt with a green scarf around its neck. A green baseball cap that had been splashed with red paint was stuffed on top of its featureless face. It was Charles, she was sure of it, trying to scare her. Imitating gang colors, from her old school in a tough neighborhood.

She couldn't believe the nerve of him, putting a mannequin on her deck. She didn't like him coming up her steps, touching her table, smelling her flowers—

Stop it Juliet, don't get crazy about this. He's only trying to scare you. She left the evil doll where she found it, unlocked the back door, and went inside her house. Her home was quiet and peaceful, but her hands were shaking. Should she call Lois and see what the police could do?

She went into the bathroom quickly and as she had done a hundred times before, looked behind the shower curtain and in the linen closet. She had watched *Psycho* too many times as a kid. She pinched herself for being a baby and a fool but she kept on looking under beds and behind doors.

She splashed some water on her face. She looked tired. Too much champagne and too little sleep? Too much love and not enough laughter? She went out into the living room and played a few chords on the piano. *You'd be so easy to love.* Well, he would be easy to love.

She went back outside. What to do with her uninvited house guest? She supposed she could drop the dummy over the side of the deck, but she didn't want to touch it. It gave her a creepy feeling like her hands would be stained irrevocably. She looked at the wannabe gang dummy again and shivered. *A plague on both your houses.* Why couldn't Charles just go away and leave her alone?

She was still staring at the dummy when she heard his voice.

"How doth my lady? How fares my Juliet? For nothing can be ill if she be well."

Juliet looked over the side of the deck at her pirate Romeo.

"What happened to your date?" she asked him softly, blocking his view of the mannequin with her body.

"I *didn't* have a date," he said frowning. "Can I come up, Juliet? It's late and I'm tired and I want to hold you in my arms."

"Shh! Be quiet, someone will hear you," she admonished, but felt the warmth of his desire rising up like a caress.

"Who cares? I don't care who sees us." He raised his hand over his head, the other held the book, their script of love. *"I defy you, stars!"* he shouted.

"Be quiet!" she ordered. "Do you carry that book with you everywhere? Go back home to your sons or Veronica or to any other little girl you take to French bistros and stuff with escargot and ply with liquor."

"She told you, did she? I only took her out because my kids said I was over the hill and getting decrepit."

"I see," she said coolly. "Do you and your sons share dates often? Do you compare notes on the women you take out and take to bed?"

"Hey, my boys are good kids, they're only twenty-one. They don't sleep with girls."

"Right," she said.

"Well, not often, anyway, they're too busy making money and playing sports. Raising hell, too," he grinned.

"Like father, like sons," she quoted.

"I like to raise hell now and then, you won't hold that against me, Juliet, will you? Come on honey, can I come up? I'd climb up but I'm dog tired after working all day."

He looked so sure of himself. Standing there in the half shadows of the alley lights he looked about twenty-one. She wondered if he had taken Veronica or any other young woman to bed and felt pangs of intense jealousy. She was moved to exact revenge. She stepped aside and waved a hand in the direction of her silent intruder.

"I'd like to ask you up, James, but as you see, I've got company."

He squinted in the light. He saw the outline of a man's form and frowned. "Why didn't you tell me you had somebody over? Why did you tell me to come over here at all if you had a... guest?"

"Did I tell you to come over?" she inquired vaguely. "I don't remember, it must have been the champagne that made me forget."

"Maybe you're having a senior moment," he said with an angry laugh.

"Getting Alzheimer's?" she asked coldly.

"Something like that," he said. "Who is this guy, anyway?"

"A fellow professor from school." she lied.

"Oh, I see, you can mix metaphors with your martinis. Discuss Shakespeare and pop Prozac while you discuss your papers."

"I don't take Prozac," she said, feeling annoyed.

"Well, I should, 'cause you're getting me depressed." He scuffed his toe into the grass like a little boy. "Well baby, if you're busy, I'm going to be on my way. But I've got to say this, Juliet honey, you sure do work fast. I guess experience is a great teacher after all." He stomped off down the alley and she watched his broad back retreating to his Jeep.

Damn, she thought. He's gone. And I'm alone. He gunned his red Jeep down the alley like a kid. She watched the taillights fade away, until the tiny lights flickered and vanished.

Who got taught the lesson tonight, Juliet? She asked herself that question and stomped off to her chaste, white bed.

CHAPTER TEN

JULIET WOKE UP TO THE SOUNDS OF HER NEIGHBORHOOD. THE singing birds, the sound of the elevated train running in the distance, her neighbor's lawnmower, and barking beagles were her morning reveille.

She pulled the covers over her head. *Get up, you have work to do.*

If she could only get through the day, go grocery shopping, prepare a test, workout, and keep her mind off a certain gorgeous man, then she would be fine. She threw off the blanket and stomped off to the bathroom. She was wearing her Rolling Stones t-shirt and boxer shorts that a student had brought her from London, and her hair was messy waves from sleep and last night's overabundance of mousse. She looked at herself in the mirror. She felt like Dracula's mother.

She walked barefoot into the kitchen, made coffee, checked the mail and read a postcard from her daughter while she waited for the dark roast to brew. 'Paris is lovely,' her daughter wrote, 'wish you were here.' Did she wish she was in Paris? You bet, with a certain someone. She had never been to Paris with a lover. That was one of the things she had put on her list of life goals a long time ago.

She walked out on her deck and saw two bodies sitting at her pine table. She almost dropped the cup. One was the dummy from the night before, the other was wearing a camouflage shirt and ripped shorts and dirty sneakers.

"That coffee smells good," he said to her, looking her up and down. "Mind if I get a cup for me and my friend?"

She stared at him open-mouthed, blinking a little in the strong sunlight.

"Good morning, Miss teacher, good morning to you," he half sing-songed with a grin.

"What are you doing here?" she asked, pulling out her shirt a little to hide her bosom.

He caught the gesture and grinned again appreciatively.

"I came back to give you a piece of my mind," he said, "and I guess I wanted to see if that dude had spent the night. I was so jealous after I left you, I almost got into a fight."

"Really?" she sat down at the table with her coffee, fascinated at his intensity. *A fight over her.*

"Yeah, some guy was trying to tell me that Michael Jordan wasn't a great basketball player, only lucky, and I had to straighten him out a little." He laughed. "So, I did."

"Was this in a tavern by any chance?" she inquired sweetly.

"I stopped for a short beer after I left you, how could I sleep knowing you were up here with some other guy?" He looked at the mannequin slumped in the chair and grimaced. "Friend of yours? Another warning?"

"Of course not," she lied, "I use it in one of my classes."

He stared at her. "Liar. This was another scare from your student. He's trying to act like a rich boy gangbanger. He's trying to scare you."

"He will go away," she said firmly. "He'll move on."

Jim looked at her thoughtfully.

"There's trouble everywhere, Miss teacher lady, you know that. After all your years teaching in the inner city you still seem so innocent, so naive. You're so untouched by trouble." He sighed. "I guess that's one of the reasons I love you so."

"I like to believe in the goodness of people," she said.

"Even me?"

She took a sip of coffee.

"You're really mad at me because of last night, aren't you?" he asked.

"It's hard to believe a man when he's in one lady's bed on Tuesday and escorting a younger lady two days later," she said.

"That's what my kids say, I play around too much." He picked up the arm of the latex doll and let it fall with a thump. "I'm going to get a cup of coffee, if you don't mind." He stomped off to the kitchen.

Juliet looked up at the sun and the sky. She hoped the morning light was kind to her complexion, with no make-up to protect it.

"Are you tired?" she asked him when he came back. "You've had a rough week."

"I know," he yawned. "I've been up rescuing damsels from parking lots and escorting girls to cocktail parties and laying pipes under a house. Nothing special. I even got to make love to a gorgeous woman this week, but that was a long time ago." He stared at her and her face burned with the memory of his kisses.

"I know," she said at last, "everything happens so fast around here."

He pointed to the mannequin. "Should we take it down to the police station?"

"No, just get rid of it," she said.

"I will do that," he said. "It must be hard to concentrate when you have two dummies to talk to."

He picked up the mannequin and carried it down the stairs.

She heard the lid of the dumpster opening and closing in the alley.

"We should have kept it and shown it to the police," he said, taking a big gulp of coffee. "Hmm, delish, you make good coffee. Miss Juliet."

"No, it's fine, it was just another joke. I'm glad you threw it away. And I'm glad you like my coffee."

"If we're going to spend a lot of mornings together, we should at least agree on coffee," he said.

He took his keys and the pink Penguin book of Romeo and Juliet out of his back pocket. He stretched his body and grinned at her.

"Got time for a little nap, Juliet? I could go back to sleep, right now," his voice dropped to a deep whisper, "with you."

Yes, let's go, her mind shouted, but she smiled sweetly and said, "I'm going to yoga this morning. Want to meditate with me?"

He picked up the book and ruffled pages. *"Not I, believe me. You have dancing shoes with nimble soles; I have a soul of lead so stakes me to the ground, I cannot move."*

"You are a lover," she quoted back. *"Borrow Cupid's wings and soar with them above a common bound."*

He reached out his hand invitingly. "All right, Juliet, let's soar together then."

She stood up and pulled at her clothes. "I didn't mean—I mean, I was just following your quote. Dammit, you get me so flustered."

"You weren't inviting me to your bed? Too bad." He smiled with unabashed good humor. "Flustered is a good word. I gotta remember that one. Wanna ride to yoga, pretty lady?"

She let out a sigh. "Let me change my clothes and I'll get my mat and my bag," she said.

"Wanna ride home?"

"It's only a mile, I'll walk, I need the exercise."

"Suit yourself," he smiled. "I'm gonna get more coffee, to take with me. I'll return the cup, you can trust me."

"I'm sure I can," she said.

The red Jeep was in the alley purring seductively when she came out of her house, walking through the back yard, enjoying the fragrant rose bushes and day lilies.

"Nice car," she said, as he opened the door for her. "Is it true that men who drive big red cars are the fastest drivers?"

"The fastest and the best, baby," he smiled. "We drive fast, we work hard, we love hard."

"Hmmmm," she said, and looked out the window. They drove in silence, and she hoped he couldn't hear the restless beating of her heart. He pulled up in front of the studio.

"Want to pose with me?" she invited. "Come inside."

"Wish I could," he said. "But I gotta work. Always gotta work. What is it, today; cows and downward dogs?" He looked at her body and sighed.

"Both," she said, feeling a warmth in her lower regions. "And you seem to know your yoga poses."

"I've been around," he said. "But I gotta go to work." He looked at her with regret. "But since you wouldn't soar with me and I can't pose with you, at least promise me you'll go out with me tonight."

She couldn't have said no if the entire literature department forbade her. "What did you have in mind?"

"Dinner, dancing, hugging, kissing—"

"I get the idea," she said, "but—"

"We don't have to sleep together, if you don't want to, but let's have dinner and be close. What's wrong with that? What's wrong with wanting to feel alive? I'd like to get to know you better, Juliet. And I want you to get to like me. What's wrong with that?" he repeated.

"I do like you," she said.

"How about love and trust?" he asked.

"Ah," said Juliet, "that's a different story."

"I do love you, Juliet," he said. "I wish you'd believe that. So how about dinner tonight?"

"Okay, I'd love to," she practically cooed, and scooted out of the car.

She went to the studio and stretched and meditated, trying to curb her restlessness and her growing need for him. After a brisk walk home for her car she went over to her daughter's house and cut the grass and watered the plants. Then she did the same at her own home. She worked quickly, eagerly awaiting the evening and felt the anticipation that energized her every movement.

A real date with a real man, it had been so long. She forced herself to lie down, drank peppermint iced tea and put soothing chamomile herbal packs around her eyes. She took her mood enhancing vitamins and tried to breathe like a yoga master.

Too bad I can't recharge myself like a battery pack, she thought, trying to sleep. He's got enough energy for three people.

After an hour of trying to rest she got up, showered, shaved, plucked, massaged and creamed her entire body. In the mirror, she studied her face. On a good day she looked forty-five, on a bad one she looked like an unearthed mummy, fresh from King Tut's tomb.

Quit it, you're in great shape.

But I'm fifty-five, she thought. I have ten extra years of crow's feet around my eyes. And when gravity hits and my breasts start to tilt down to the floor will he be so turned on then?

He arrived five minutes early, all dressed up and, surprisingly, at the front door. He was wearing an ivory linen jacket, cobalt blue silk shirt that matched his eyes, trim khaki trousers and navy-blue boots. In his hand, he held one white rose.

"For you, Miss teacher lady," he said and kissed her cheek. "How goes my Juliet?"

"Well, thank you," she said softly, holding the rose up to her face. "Thank you for the flower. White roses are my favorite." The aroma was delicate and tickled her nostrils.

"*Verona hath not such a flower*," he misquoted, his eyes full of love. He looked at her in her flowing white dress that was draped off one tanned shoulder. "You look like a Greek goddess tonight, Juliet. The goddess of the moon and love."

"And you look very handsome," she replied. She looked downwards. "My goodness, your boots! Are those stars and moons?"

He stuck out one expensive, hand-tooled boot.

"Hand-made in Mexico," he said. "Do you approve?"

She nodded and he draped her silk shawl around her shoulders. She experienced a *frisson* of electric current run through her veins at his touch.

She carried the rose and a small gold clutch purse in one hand, he firmly held the other.

He escorted her to a red Mustang.

"No Jeep?" she asked.

"No, this is my date car," he said, with a smile.

"I see, do young ladies go for this?" she looked around the customized car with ivory leather seats, a superb stereo system and a vanity mirror lighted by pink and white hearts.

"Yeah, they go for it," he said and expertly drove them to their destination.

"I forgot to ask you, you're not a vegetarian, are you, Juliet? I want to take you to my favorite place, it's Cajun. Crawfish and lobsters and fantastic barbeque. And, a really great band."

"Sounds like fun," she said.

It *was* fun. They drank strawberry margaritas and ate Caesar salad, popcorn shrimp and hickory smoked chicken and ribs. They danced to the *Tennessee Waltz* and to *Jambalaya* played by a tremendous Zydeco band. James was a strong, solid dancer and when he swung her around and caught her up close in his arms, she felt every sinew and lean curve of his body pressing against the thin silk of her dress.

"Everything all right? Are you having a good time?" he murmured into her ear.

"I'm having a wonderful time," she said.

He kissed her lightly under her ear and then swooped in to claim her mouth. Time stood still, the accordion music was suspended, as their lips met in a sweet kiss. She lost her step and he held her tenderly for a moment.

"Let's sit down," he said softly.

She nodded in agreement. He led her back to their comfortable booth, far enough away from the music so they could talk.

"Do you want anything else, Juliet?" he asked her. "Another drink?"

"No, everything was delicious. I haven't been on much of a diet since I met you."

"You're in perfect shape," he assured her. "You don't want to become too thin, do you? Women should look like women, and you Juliet," his voice dropped an octave, "feel and look like a woman."

"Dessert?" the waiter asked.

"No, thanks," Jim said, looking straight at Juliet, "I'll have mine at home."

She was glad it was dark enough so they couldn't see her blush. They started to leave the crowded restaurant, passing through the bar which was three-deep in customers.

"Hey, Dad!" a voice said.

"Randy, what's up?" Father and son performed a perfect high five.

Juliet watched them. Two blond pirates, booted and with earrings, boldly surveying the social seas. A senior and junior pirate who could hold their own.

"Juliet, this is my son, Randy. Randy, this is Mrs. West."

"Nice to meet you, Mrs. West," the young man said politely, shaking her hand.

"And it's nice to meet you," Juliet said. "I've heard so much about you and your brother. Do you both look just like your dad?"

"No, I'm better looking than both of them," Randy laughed.

"Are you alone tonight?" Jim asked his son.

"No, I'm waiting for a lady."

"I like your boots," Juliet said, looking at his grey leather ones with sky blue scroll work. "Do the three of you share shoes?"

"No, only women," Jim said with an innocent look at her.

Now she pinched him above the elbow.

"Ouch," James said, and pulled her close to him, grabbing her hand. His son watched the interplay with interest.

"Actually, Dad and I are the wild ones. My brother Mike thinks he's a preppy because he wears Brooks Brothers duds and Gucci loafers."

"He wants to be an investment counselor," Jim said with pride.

"Mike is the brains of the family," Randy said easily.

"You're smart," his father said. "Who runs the company for me most of the time? Especially now that I've got homework to do."

"Yeah, make him write a lot of papers, Mrs. West," Randy said. "He needs the work."

"I will," Juliet promised.

"Behave yourself, son," Jim said, placing his arm around Juliet's shoulders.

"And you too, Pop," his son smiled. "It was a pleasure meeting you, Mrs. West."

"Charming boy," she said to Jim. "And he's so handsome."

"They're both good boys," he said softly. "They really kept me alive after Barbara died."

"I'm sure they did," she said. "You must miss her terribly." They walked to the car hand in hand.

"I do, I did," he said squeezing her fingers gently, "but lately I've been feeling a whole lot better about myself."

"I know what you mean, it's like one day you wake up and suddenly everything seems bright and new like it's been covered with a fresh coat of paint," she said.

"More metaphors, Miss teacher lady?" he laughed. "But speaking of paint, I still think you should report that kid. It's a hell of a nerve having him come to your home making a mess and leaving that stupid dummy at your table."

"I know, you're right," she sighed. She didn't want him to know the whole story. "But let's not talk about it right now. Let's enjoy the evening. It's been so wonderful."

He pulled up to her house. "Is there room in your garage for my car?"

"Your chariot? Of course," she said. She handed him the keys. He looked at her and hesitated.

"I'm inviting myself to spend the night," he said softly.

"I know you are," she said.

He traced a finger up and down her arm.

"Is it okay if I sleep beside you tonight? I won't do anything you don't want me to."

She cleared her throat. *Do everything,* she thought.

"You can stay," she said. "I want you to stay."

"Tempt not a desperate man," he quoted. The garage door began to slowly open.

"You certainly have learned your Shakespeare," she said in awe.

"I read R and J a lot when I'm on the job waiting for things to happen or for clients to show up. It comforts me and it makes me feel close to you, Juliet."

Her heart lurched. Were these the words of a reckless playboy? Did he guess the effect his confession was having on her nervous system?

"James Sanders," she sighed. "You are such a romantic."

"Does that mean you're finally falling in love with me?" he asked.

Say it, how can it hurt?

"If thou think'st I am too quickly won, I'll frown and be perverse and say thee nay," she quoted softly, stalling for time, *"so thou wilt woo, but... in truth, fair Montague,"* she said, *"I am too fond."*

He parked the car and moved in closer to her. "Go ahead, you can say it, Juliet," he urged in a husky voice. "Tell me how you feel."

She licked her lips and tried to form the words. *Just say it, I love you. You'll feel better.* But she hadn't said those words to a man in many years—over ten years—and her heart was so afraid.

"I'm afraid," she said.

"I'll help you," he whispered and gently put his fingers up to her lips. "Whisper it, I'll take it from your mouth and put it to my heart," he said. "Just say, 'I love you, James'."

"I," she started to whisper. "I," she looked out the window and jumped. "I see a man!" she said loudly. "My God, there's somebody here!"

CHAPTER ELEVEN

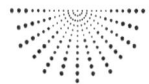

Jim jumped out of the car.

"Who is it?" he shouted. "Who's there?"

Juliet held her breath. It couldn't be Charles could it? What if he was armed and high on drugs. He wouldn't know Jim at all. And Jim could get hurt. She quickly opened the door and got out with a pounding heart. She switched on the light.

A familiar face was standing there in front of her.

"Charles!" Juliet was shocked. "What are you doing here?"

He smiled innocently. Juliet felt her stomach clench with dread.

"I'm sorry, Mrs. West, I didn't mean to scare you and your friend. I was waiting for you, to see if you would come home tonight."

"In the garage?" Jim asked, still suspicious.

"I didn't want to sit on your deck, Mrs. West, you know you got that nosy neighbor next door and I didn't want to make her nervous."

"So, what do you want?" She cleared her throat, she felt anger, mixed with apprehension.

"Believe it or not," he said, "the police still think I have something to do with that missing book, and I said you would vouch for me."

"I already did once," she said coldly. "Why do I need to again?"

"You know how the police are," Charles shrugged, "so untrusting. And all that unfinished business." He giggled and Juliet again wondered if he was high on drugs.

"What business?" Jim asked, folding his arms across his broad chest. "I hope this doesn't include Mrs. West, this business. I'm Jim Sanders, a good friend of hers."

Charles shook his hand respectfully. "No, it doesn't, the police were curious about that book and some other stuff that was—missing." The young man looked the same, but his attitude and posture was different. He seemed smug with a tinge of defiance. He was neatly dressed in khakis and a polo shirt, and his hair was in a clipped, short respectable hairstyle. He looked like the college student that he was supposed to be. Yet, the look in his face was disturbing.

"What can I do for you tonight?" Juliet asked. "Maybe you should come see me at school one afternoon and we can discuss your situation."

"Situation," he laughed, but to her ears it sounded like a sneer. "Yeah, I'll come to school and we can discuss my situation."

"Email me first," she said. "So we can set up an appointment."

"Great idea," he said and smirked again.

"Maybe it's time you went home, son," Jim said, with a disapproving look.

"Yeah, I get it, I'm not wanted here," Charles said.

"I'll see you at school," Juliet said firmly.

"Sure, I can do that," he said. "But I need a place to crash tonight, can you help me out?"

"Help you—help you out? Why? Don't you have a place to stay?"

"Well, you know my family, they are so uptight, I can't go home when they think I'm in trouble with the cops."

"So, you have nowhere to stay," she said.

His blue eyes burned into her dark ones. *I got something on you lady, I can make trouble.*

"Okay, one night, you can stay here," she said. "But I want you to talk to your family in the morning."

"Will do," Charles said lazily.

"Let's go in," Juliet said with a shiver. "It's getting chilly."

Charles went to the bathroom and Jim grabbed her by the shoulders.

"What the hell are you doing?"

"I'm sorry," Juliet said to Jim, "but what could I do? I couldn't let him go off into the night with nowhere to go. It would be like—"

"Child abuse?" Jim asked with a frown. "'Cause, lady, he looks like a beat-up child, and up to no good."

"He does have a strange look about him," she agreed. "But I'm sure he can get things straightened out with his family. I've met his parents, they seemed supportive."

"You believe him?" Jim asked her. "There's stuff he's not telling you, I bet."

"Yes," she said. "I do, more or less." She didn't want to explain. Not tonight.

"Great," Jim said, and lay down on the sofa.

"What are you doing?" Juliet asked him with a frown.

"What does it look like, honey? I'm going to sleep here all night on your lovely but lumpy sofa to protect your honor and keep you safe from any more wandering criminals who might show up."

Charles emerged from the bathroom. He was yawning and he looked like he had scrubbed his face.

"Do you feel better?" Juliet asked him.

"Yes, thanks," he yawned again, and stretched.

"You'd better go to sleep," Juliet said. "You've got to go home tomorrow. And talk to your family."

"That's an idea," he giggled again. "Talk to the old parents? When have they ever listened to me?"

"Let me talk to them," Juliet said. "The truth is better than lies and hiding."

"I'll think about it." Charles sighed, shaking his head. "I don't want to get packed off to New York again."

"We can talk to them tomorrow, you can explain about the book and wanting to make restitution and I am sure with a good attorney, things will be okay."

"You sure have everything all planned out for me, don't you? Like I said, I'll think about it. Where do I sleep?"

She walked him into the guest room. "Here, it should be comfortable. Get some rest, you look tired."

He plopped down on the bed. "Nice and soft," he said and threw his arms over his head and closed his eyes. She stared at him for a moment and then turned off the light.

When she came out of the room she saw Jim staring at her, deep in thought. "You don't have to stay here on the couch," she said.

"I don't? Are you sure he won't hear anything through the wall?" he smiled at her.

"That's not what I meant," she said, with a sigh of exasperation. "Must you always think about sex?"

"Where you're concerned, it's hard not to think about it, lady," he said.

Juliet's stomach lurched with wanting him. "Don't think about it," she advised. "It helps to keep your mind off it, if you're trying to be celibate."

"Thanks for the advice," he said and rolled over with a groan. "Aw, Juliet, you're such a beauty tonight and I've been longing, burning up to hold you in my arms. Now, I'm back on this couch with a pillow for a substitute." He rolled the pillow up in his arms and put his head on it. His golden earring glittered in the light.

"Do you ever take that earring off?" she asked, sitting down beside him.

"Sometimes," he said, trailing a finger down her bare arm. "Do you ever take this off?" He tugged lightly at her dress.

"Only in the privacy of my own room," she said.

"Too bad," he said and pulled her down to him.

He kissed her deeply and with the warmth of his pent-up passions. She responded with her own desire and with a regret that she had been feeling ever since she discovered Charles in the garage. Wanting Jim, being so close to him and feeling the sweet, tantalizing frustration of their inability to express their need for each other was so disappointing. His hands were warm and gentle on her back, her breasts ached for him, and when she finally tore her lips away and buried her face in the curve of his neck, she felt his pulse beat wildly.

"Juliet," he moaned, "take me to your bed, just for a little while."

"Tomorrow night," she promised. "Tomorrow."

"Parting is such sweet sorrow, that I shall say good night 'til it be morrow," he quoted huskily.

"Goodnight," she said shakily. *"Sleep dwell upon thine eyes, peace in thy breast,"* she said, looking down at him with regret.

"I don't know about peace," he said with a grunt, tugging at his trousers. "Have you got a shirt and shorts for me, Juliet? I hate sleeping in these clothes, I can't move." She went into her bedroom and returned with a Chicago Bears shirt and work out shorts that belonged to her son-in-law. Without a word he tore off his silk and khakis and put on the clothes. She stared at his muscles, his tattoo and his beautiful strong back. He lay down again and grinned at her. "How am I doing?" he asked. "Am I okay for a old man?"

"You are doing very well indeed," Juliet sighed, "absolutely wonderful."

"Thank you, ma'am," he stared up at her standing there, all

dark eyes and red lips from his kisses, her provocative white dress caressing her body like doves flying around her curves. "You're also the stuff of dreams."

She went into her bedroom and changed. She could hear him whistling a little tune and it thrilled her.

"Juliet?" he called softly.

"Yes?" she walked back in the dimly lit room, wearing her pink nightgown and slippers.

"Gee, you're pretty," he said appreciatively.

"Is that what you wanted to tell me?" she asked.

"No, it's about Charles," Jim dropped his voice. "You know you've got to call his parents tomorrow. You can't give him money."

"I know," she said, "I was just trying keep him calm by agreeing with him." *And trying to figure out if he really had pictures of them together. Him falling into her arms? She couldn't remember.*

"You can call your friend Lois in the morning and get some advice," he advised. "She was a cop. You know and trust her. And it sounds like his parents can afford a lawyer. These rich kids always get off without doing time."

She was staring at him thoughtfully.

"Right, honey? You do agree with me, right?"

"Right," she said softly. "Okay, James. Don't you want to call your sons and let them know where you are?"

He smiled into the pillow. "They know where I am, Juliet. Especially after Randy met you tonight. Good night, baby."

"Good night," she answered. How she was ever going to get a wink of sleep tonight, she had no clue.

CHAPTER TWELVE

Juliet woke up to the rich, strong aroma of coffee and the sound of laughter. She stretched luxuriously and ran her hands up and down her torso. Soft, generous curves, still unfulfilled from last night. Oh, how she wanted her Romeo and oh, how he had been denied to her by the strange twists of fate.

Hey, you're a grown up, she told herself. *Get with the program.*

She put on her robe and slippers and combed her hair. She inspected her face quickly. Not too bad in the dawn's early light, but she was no American Beauty rose after a night of barbeque and margaritas.

She opened the door to her bedroom. She was glad Charles and Jim were getting along. He was basically a good kid, and she hoped Jim would figure that out over breakfast.

"Hi, honey," Jim smiled at her. He was barefoot and looked enormously male in his too-small borrowed clothing. He had a red and white gingham apron around his taut middle and had a rapt audience of two watching him skillfully turn pancakes on the griddle. Lois was drinking coffee and Beatrice was staring at him in adoration. They all looked absolutely chummy, Juliet decided.

He walked up to Juliet and kissed her cheek.

"Hi, Miss teacher lady," he said and gallantly pulled out a chair for her. "How do you like your coffee?" He picked up the pot and began to pour. "I'm just starting to get to know her likes and dislikes," he confided to the women with a boyish grin.

"Aren't we laying it on just a little thick this morning?" she asked him sweetly.

He stared at her innocently with his hand hovering over the sugar bowl.

"What do you mean?" he asked.

"Just cream, please, darling," she cooed. "No sugar."

"She's sweet enough," he said to the girls. "She only likes it in her iced tea."

"How wonderful to have such an attentive beau," Lois said and smiled.

"I know," Beatrice sighed. "I never meet anybody who remembers what I like."

"James *doth teach the torches to burn bright*," Juliet said. "*Beauty too rich for use, for earth too dear*." In response he bowed and expertly flipped a pancake on her plate.

"*Did my heart love till now?*" he said with a twinkle in his eye. "*For I ne'er saw true beauty til this night*. Or morning," he amended, and placed a very nice tan pancake in front of Lois.

"A man who quotes poetry and cooks, where did you find him, Juliet?" Lois asked.

"I don't know, I guess it was in the stars," she said with a look at Jim who stood there, enjoying himself.

"Ain't it nice to have a man around the house?" he asked with a grin.

Juliet almost choked on her coffee. "Where's Charles?"

"He's gone, Juliet," Lois said, shaking her head. "Jim saw me this morning working in my yard and came over to tell me about the young man who stayed the night."

"Gone?" she repeated. "It's only seven o'clock."

"I got up early," he said. "I checked the guest bedroom but he was gone. I wasn't surprised, he must have climbed out the window. So, I went outside and looked around and then watched the sunrise. Pretty," he smiled at her. *"It is the east and Juliet is the sun."*

"This is like a movie," Beatrice said enviously.

"Which one?" Juliet said in annoyance, looking at his smug face. "The Exorcist? The Wizard of Oz?"

"No munchkins around here, Juliet," Lois said. "Only disappearing young men, it seems."

"Anyway, after I saw he had vamoosed, I went in to check on you, sweetheart," he said, "to make sure you were all right. I mean I knew you were all right," he stretched his body like a panther and exhaled a big gulp of air. "Two were in their beds last night. I was on the couch." He put a hand to heart in mock disappointment. "Ah, me. I was devastated."

Beatrice giggled again. "You look just like Mike," she beamed. "I dated Mike during my junior year in high school. And then I hung out with Randy last year—we were both working the Toys for Tots holiday event."

And Papa? Juliet raised her eyebrows at Jim but he only grinned back and silently raised his coffee cup in tribute.

"This is all so fascinating," she said. "But where did Charles go? Did he go home? Did he leave a note?"

"No note. He's gone. He split, he disappeared," Jim said.

"I didn't hear him leaving, not a sound. I was dead to the world," Juliet said.

"I guess he's good at sneaking around," Jim said with a frown. "Sorry, Juliet, but it seems he's not the good kid you thought he was."

Juliet grabbed her coffee and marched out of the kitchen. She went to the guest bedroom and did a fast inspection. She found no traces of Charles. She looked out the window and thought she saw a footprint in the bushes, but she couldn't tell for sure.

"See anything?" Jim was leaning up against the door watching her. "Any clues? Are you Sherlock Holmes this morning?"

"Not today," she sank down on the bed dejectedly. "Are you my Dr. Watson? You know, I can't think straight. I can't believe he ran away, before we had a chance to talk."

"Guilty conscience?" Jim asked. "Or does he want to sort out his own issues? You tell me, he was your student."

Lois stuck her head in the doorway. "Did you find anything, Jule? Any notes?"

"Nothing," she said. "I guess he went home."

"Would you like me to do anything? Ask my friends at the station to do a background check on him?"

"I guess you could," Juliet said. "Maybe I'll hear from him later today."

Beatrice appeared. "I've got to go to the library and do my homework." She looked at Jim again with frank admiration and at Juliet with respect. "It was nice meeting you," she said to Jim.

"Likewise," he said. "It's so cool that Juliet has such great neighbors."

Beatrice blushed. "Be careful, Juliet. Don't stay so long at school at night by yourself."

"She will be careful," Jim said, placing his hands on Juliet's shoulders. Beatrice and Lois left with promises to check in on her later.

Juliet was deep in thought. She looked around the room. She got up and opened the top dresser drawer. Inside were things that belonged to her daughter. Girl Scout patches and a Barbie doll of some value and silver jewelry that she had bought in Mexico. She also possessed a collection of crosses from around the world. Some of the crosses were gold and from Greece, others were from Turkey, Macedonia and Italy. A few were silver and from Mexico and South America. Colette had stored them in a purple velvet bag and had planned to take them home after her vacation. Juliet picked up a silk scarf and frowned. The bag had vanished.

"Something wrong?" Jim asked her. "Is there something missing?"

"No, nothing," Juliet turned to him with a smile. "I was just looking at my daughter's things."

"Come finish your breakfast," he said. "I want to talk to you before I have to go."

"Must you leave so early?" Juliet had hoped that he could stay, maybe even take a little nap.

"I promised my sons I would drive up to Michigan with them to look at a boat today," he said. "I don't want to leave you, Juliet," he said, putting his hand up to gently stroke her face. "I don't like leaving you alone."

"I'll be all right, nothing is going to happen." But she thought of the missing gold crosses and knew the culprit was Charles.

"I know what, Juliet. Come with me, today. Let me take you away for the rest of the weekend. It will be fun. We can go swimming and water skiing, parasailing if you like."

"No bungee jumping?" she asked with a smile.

"You're into that, too?" he asked. "That can be arranged. But only if we get tied up to each other and jump."

Juliet delicately shuddered. "I am way, way too old for that. I was joking."

"On second thought, I'd just like to get tied up to you, period," he said with a frank look that sent her pulses racing. "Come on, Juliet, my sons would love to have you along. You're a lot of fun."

"I don't want to intrude on your weekend with your boys. I'm sure you don't get to spend that much time with them, these days. And besides, I should work," she said with a sigh. "I have a curriculum report to prepare and I am working on a book with a deadline."

"Your poetry, right?" he asked.

"Yes, and it's not just me, there's a lot of women counting on me to get this book published. It will be another credential for them."

"You are so dutiful, Miss teacher lady," he said and stroked her arm.

Her arm sizzled with his touch. She stared at his tattoo, the rose between the stars. If she tried to touch the rose, would she be pricked by its thorns?

"I understand," he said, "but I don't like it. I don't like leaving you here alone with kids showing up late at night in your garage and I don't like leaving you when I am dying to hold you and make love to you. *Tempt not a desperate man*, Juliet."

She swallowed hard. "You're not desperate," she said lightly. "You'll be back tomorrow and we can pick up where we left off."

"I might not be able to remember," he said, and pulled her to her feet. He put his arms around her and claimed her mouth for a passionate kiss. He was tender at first but then all their frustration of the night before broke through and he kissed her more deeply and with a strength that immobilized her in his arms. She responded with pent-up emotions that shocked and disturbed her because it spoke of needs that she had thought were long buried. He ran his hands up and down her body, she clung on to him like rambling roses up a vine, she felt the heat of his body and his manhood through the thin cotton of her nightgown.

"You won't forget," she said shakily, when they came up for air. "And neither will I."

He went into the bathroom and came out fully dressed, hair combed, boots on and smiling.

"You have my number. Call me anytime day or night if you need me or something happens." He walked over to her and put his hand under her chin. She looked up at him, the pirate Romeo, the urban Hercules, and she wished she could go away with him.

Why not? You can always work, she told herself. But her sense of self-preservation and caution was so strong and she wanted to take this a little slower. Right now, she was racing recklessly on an uncharted path of sizzling passion. She didn't want to burn up.

"Another time, I'll come with you, I promise," she said, feeling vulnerable and very young under his eyes.

"I wish you would come today," he said.

"I can't come with you," she repeated. "I've got work to do."

"No, you can, but you won't. There's a big difference," he said with a frown. "You're playing some emotional game with yourself. You don't want to admit you're human." He leaned in and nibbled a little on her trembling lower lip. "Or admit you're a woman."

"I am not in a state of denial," she said, expelling a shaky breath. "I know exactly who I am."

"And who is that, Mrs. Wild, Wild West?"

"I'm a teacher, a grandmother and a woman living alone. I was married for twenty-five years to a man, a nice enough man but a weak man, who gambled and lied and ran up debts that I am still paying off."

"You could have declared bankruptcy," he said. "It's done all the time."

"But not by me!" she said with anger. "I didn't want to have to re-establish my credit or lose my house," she said. "It's hard to start over at fifty. I've had to reinvent myself and it wasn't easy." She walked away and stood looking out the window. The day was so bright but she felt so dark inside.

"I had to invent myself at forty when my wife died," Jim said softly. "I've been wild but I haven't buried myself in schoolwork and yoga, like you, Juliet. I'm a risk taker. It's the only way to get someplace."

"I'm not buried. I met you two weeks ago and already we've been to bed. Isn't that a risk?" she demanded. She ached for his touch but stood with her arms wrapped around her stomach, not daring to move.

His tanned, rugged face was serious.

"I don't call it a risk," he said. "I call it falling in love. I call it wonderful."

"I didn't mean it wasn't nice, James," she said. "Really, I didn't."

"Nice? All this passion and poetry and me going nuts over you, you call that nice? That's all?" He pulled at his hair in frustration.

"Of course not, it's more than nice. You know what I mean. I just wanted to take this slowly. I didn't want to rush into anything that we couldn't handle gracefully."

"I can handle you," he said with a ghost of a smile tugging at the corner of his sensuous mouth.

"Relationships are about more than sex," she insisted. "There's trust, and mutual respect and family."

"I want to meet your family and I want you to meet mine," he said, with a funny look. "Or ain't I good enough for you? I don't talk so refined and I got a tattoo, Miss teacher lady. And I don't like phonies."

"Are you calling me a phony?" she demanded.

"You know I was afraid to enroll in college. I thought I was too dumb. I picked your college because it had a good continuing ed program and my sons told me to try it. So, I tried it. I was so nervous, I almost quit the first day. How do you like that? Me, the Marine, the guy who never passed up a fight, being afraid of literature and learning. But when I walked in and saw all the books and desks and smelled that clean smell—I don't know what it is, maybe the smell of lysol and education and knowledge, and maybe even, yeah you, Miss teacher lady, I got scared."

"That's only natural," Juliet said.

"For you," he said. "You been allowed to get scared. I wasn't. My dad worked as a foreman on the steel mills on the southeast side. I was raised to be tough and never walk away from trouble. And now I gotta walk away from you."

Her eyes widened. "Gone already?" she asked softly.

"I don't mean permanently, but for the weekend. I want to be with you and I can't because you won't come with me. And I gotta be with my sons. You gotta loosen up, Juliet, and trust your heart."

"My heart wants to go but my mind is afraid," she said lightly.

"Of me?" he demanded.

"Of being hurt. Of falling in love with a man who's been around and raises hell and takes out very young babes."

"That's all over," he insisted.

"I need time," she said.

"I'm in love with you," he said, taking a step forward.

She put up her hands as if to stop a falling avalanche. "I need time."

"OK, honey, if that's what you want." He took out his copy of Romeo and Juliet from his jacket pocket. *"Too rash, too unadvised, too sudden,"* he read.

"Love moderately," she quoted back at him. "We need time to develop a relationship," she said. "Don't look so unhappy, please don't," she begged him.

"My wife and I got married seven days after we met. I guess I thought the same was true with you, Juliet. I felt lucky the first day I saw you in class. I felt blessed."

"We are blessed," she said miserably. "But I'm not your wife, I'm me, and I can't rush. It's not in my nature."

"Okay, babe, no problem," he said with a little smile that did not reach his eyes. "You've got my number, call me anytime you want to talk. Or need help." He put his hands on her shoulders. She stared resolutely at his chin.

"Juliet?"

She raised her eyes.

"I love you," he said.

She smiled wanly. "Thank you."

"Be careful," he said and opened the front door. They both blinked at the brightness. "Be careful," he repeated. "Make sure the door is always locked. Call me." He kissed her swiftly and was gone.

CHAPTER THIRTEEN

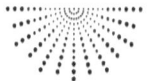

CALL ME. RATHER IMPERIOUS AND BOSSY, WASN'T HE? HE HAD BEEN very masterful in the classroom and the bedroom but that wasn't the point. He wasn't afraid of her. He wanted her to call him. His tenderness was so intense and sweet that when she was in his arms she wanted to weep with happiness. She felt so protected.

She picked up the phone. Call him. Tell him that you care. She looked at it like it was a strange alien being and swiftly put it down. *Not yet.*

The phone rang again.

"Hi, Mom, how are you?"

"Honey," she said to her daughter, "how is everything in Paris?"

"Beautiful, but now we're in Provence and I ate too much pâté de foie gras last night in a wonderful bistro. I had dreams of Monets and Manets, that I had seen in the museums." she said.

"Goose liver is a very psychedelic food," Juliet laughed. "I remember when I was a little girl at Woodstock—"

"Please, Mother, don't start," Colette begged. "You are not that old, not even close."

"True. And how are Paul and my lovely, beautiful, granddaughter?"

"They're great, Angelica is having a wonderful time chasing peacocks and feeding deer at the chateau we're staying at. This is a glorious place, Mother. I wish you were here with us. You would love it so much."

"Perhaps sometime I will," Juliet said. Could a pirate Romeo eat goose liver in a chateau in Provence?

"Mother," Colette said.

"Yes, dear?"

"Tell me about your friend."

"What friend?" Juliet said, not giving an inch on this.

"Mother," Colette sighed, "the gorgeous guy who was over the other night."

"How do you know he's gorgeous?" Juliet demanded.

"Lois' daughter told Paul's brother."

"I see," Juliet said, "the Chicago grapevine."

"Well, tell me! Are you serious about him?"

"Honey, I've only known him two weeks," she said.

"It's Jim Sanders, isn't it?" Colette asked.

"Yes, we've been out a couple of times," Juliet said lightly.

"I hear he's quite charming."

Among other things.

"Yes, he's in my literature class. We've been to dinner, that's all," Juliet said. She was an adult, did she have to explain herself?

"Lois says he's the most handsome hunk she's ever seen around there."

She would. "I respect his desire to improve himself intellectually," Juliet said loftily.

"Right, Mom, sure. We'll be home next week and we'll see about his intellect," her daughter joked.

"Don't get fresh," Juliet said.

"Too late, you raised me that way. I can't wait to see you.

France is grand," said Colette, "but there's no place like home with your loved ones."

Loved ones. Colette was so sweet; who couldn't help but love her? Now Juliet had always been more bold and independent. She wondered if she had stayed married to Tony for so long because Tony had left her alone. Except for his need for money, he had needed her very little. Not much sex or companionship. Just a husband and a father occasionally. And now it was so frightening to be needed.

The phone rang.

"Hello?" She hoped it was him.

"Uh, Mrs. West, it's me, Charles." He sounded far away, on a fuzzy cell phone.

"Where are you?" she asked.

"Somewhere around," he laughed. "You don't need to know where."

"Charles, you didn't have to sneak away," she said.

"I had people I needed to see," he replied.

"Have you been home? Have you talked to your parents?"

"Yes," he said. "I talked to them. Everything's cool."

"Why don't I believe you?"

"You have a suspicious nature, Mrs. West," he said softly. His voice chilled her soul.

She took a deep breath and tried to sound calm. "Did you by any chance borrow some things from my daughter's room?" she asked lightly.

"I took the gold, if that's what you mean, I needed cash, right away, I owed some dudes some money. Not the kind of guys to wait." His laugh had a bitter edge.

"Are you involved in drugs, Charles?"

"It's better that you don't know anything," he said.

"Are you planning to return my daughter's jewelry?" she asked.

"It's at the pawn shop, I'll mail you the ticket before I leave town," he said. "You can get your precious jewelry back."

"Charles—"

He had hung up. It was a strange story. She knew the crosses were worth several thousand dollars because of the extreme high price of gold. She knew that, because her ex-husband had pawned her mother's engagement ring once, to pay off a poker debt. She supposed she could call Lois but what was the use? He was gone and she had no proof of anything.

She was exhausted and went to sleep early. She rose at dawn and went to the sunrise service at her church. When the minister said, "blessed are the peacemakers," she thought of Jim. When she went to the studio and joined a yoga class, she thought of Jim. When she went to sit through an afternoon movie, a revival of the Blue Angel with Marlene Dietrich, she thought of Jim.

"Falling in love again, never wanted to, what am I to do, can't help it," the sultry Lola Lola sang, and Juliet longed to rush to the telephone.

Discipline, she told herself. You *can* control your urge for him like you can control a yen for sugar, pizza or beer.

She spent another restless night dreaming of pirates climbing up her deck, after jumping over rose bushes. She had not called Jim and he hadn't tried her again. She wondered if he was mad at her for not trying to reach him. He had practically commanded her to call him and she had refused. Would he come to class tomorrow night?

She taught her seminar on Victorian poetry, went to the library to research Keats and Blake and ate dinner in her office. A tuna salad sandwich, iced tea and a peach was all she needed. She had to make up for dining out and late-night snacks.

Her office was on the first floor of a red brick building which overlooked the campus quadrangle. Tall maple and catalpa trees rimmed the lawn and there were roses and lilac bushes surrounding every building. As she sat working, the rich, heady aroma of lilac caressed her nostrils. The wind blew and the sweet scent flooded her senses and changed the direction of her thoughts. Time passed quickly and the sun had set and the moon was rising in the sky. Time to go home.

"This bud of love, by summer's ripening breath," she thought and closed her eyes. She could smell his citrus cologne, imagine the warm touch of his lips, feel his hard, lean body, and for a moment she was at peace. A cool breeze passed over her hot face and then she heard the sound of an intruder.

"To sleep, perchance to dream, ay there's the rub," recited a male voice as a leg and arm emerged through the open window.

Juliet opened her eyes in shock. Was this a dream? But no, as she watched in amazement, the familiar face of Charles appeared before her.

"What are you doing here?" she asked, a feeling of fear causing her pulse to quicken. "I thought you were leaving town."

"Not yet," he said. He looked rumpled, tired and strangely keyed-up. His eyes were filled with little pinpoints of light and his hands were thrust deep in his pockets.

"Have you come to return my daughter's jewelry?" she asked him. "Or is it still at the pawn shop?"

He stared at her with scorn.

"Have you come to offer an explanation?" she continued.

"Mrs. West, you don't get it, you don't get it at all," Charles said. "You never got it, did you?"

"Get what?" she asked in annoyance. "I'm getting confused, if that's what you mean."

"I'm not the mixed up special needs kid you thought I was. You thought some strategies and interventions could straighten me out. Well, you were wrong."

"How was I wrong?"

"I was the kid my parents didn't want. The kid who trashed things at home and killed my mother's canaries, because I was angry at them. I was always angry." He closed his eyes and ground the heels of his hands against his forehead. "I could never get over it."

"Over what?"

"Get over the fact they never loved me or wanted me."

Juliet was speechless. "I am sure you were loved—are loved."

"Wrong."

"Why are you back here? I thought you were leaving town."

"I am leaving town. But not to New York. Las Vegas. I got a friend there. But I need money."

"You've already taken my jewelry," she said. "What else do you want from me?" She was angry.

"Just money."

"For what? Drugs? To pay off your bookies? I hear you are into gambling, say my friends in the police department." She was lying, she was waiting to hear back from Lois, but she wanted answers. She wanted them now.

"You don't need to know!" he shouted, and slammed his hand down on her desk. "Don't ask me any more questions and everything will be cool, I swear it." Beads of sweat were on his forehead. He looked so young and so dangerous. A small crescent scar over his eyebrow like a small comma, was an angry red against his white skin. On his wrists, there were other scars, jagged and menacing.

They stared at each other.

"I only have twenty-five dollars on me," she said.

"I need a lot more money to get out of town."

"Charles," she said, gently, "you need help. Let's go the hospital and get you checked out. You don't look well."

"No hospital, no way. I don't need a doctor giving me meds and then calling the police. I need cash, Mrs. West, and you're going to get me plenty."

"Why did you put the stuffed doll on my deck and write beware on my garage door. What was the point of that? You were trying to scare me?"

"Maybe," he said, picking up the stapler on her desk. He punched the top down nervously, ping, ping, pang, silver slivers of steel scattered over her papers.

"Why? Why try and scare me?" she demanded. "Why not come and talk to me?"

"I knew you would turn me in about the stolen book," he said, shrugging. "I knew you wouldn't understand." He laughed and it made her skin crawl. "I thought if I scared you enough, you would help me out."

"Do you even have pictures of you falling into my arms?"

He looked amused for a moment and then leaned over her menacingly. *It's like a scene from a play*, Juliet thought, watching him carefully.

"Doesn't matter now," he shrugged. "I thought if I scared you enough about your precious reputation, you would help me." He pulled a gun out of his pocket. It shone blue-black in the office light and looked cold and cruel in his trembling hand. "See this?" he waved it under her nose and then put it back in the pocket of his khaki pants. "It doesn't matter what you think about me now, I'm going to—encourage you to help me. Let's go."

"To where?" The sight of the gun had raised the hairs on the back of her neck. Her troubled young student had become a psychopath.

"We can drive through your bank. You can make a withdrawal for me."

"The banks are closed."

"Not the drive through, they're open 24/7, the cash machines. Do you think I'm that dumb?"

"I never thought you were dumb, Charles."

"Well, that's something at least," he said. "Come on, let's go."

"And if I won't go?" she asked him coolly.

He patted his pocket nervously. "You'll go or I swear I'll shoot you."

"My blood will help your problems?" she demanded.

"All of you people are my problem. My mother, father, the shrink, the social worker—all of you think I need help. My mother and father are mortified that I'm a loser. I wasn't at my auntie's in New York. They put me in a psychiatric day school for rich punks like me." He touched his pocket again. "Let's go, I'm getting tired of talking."

Agree with him. Get out of the building. Find help, her mind screamed at her.

"All right, let's go," she said at last. She picked up her bookbag and stuffed papers into it.

"Don't try anything," he warned her.

The campus was dark and peacefully silent as they left the building. The chirping of crickets and the sound of the elevated train in the distance were soothing to her jangled nerves. Somewhere in another building there was the sound of a tenor saxophone playing scales.

She inhaled a breath. What should she do? She had been so wrong about Charles.

"You drive," Charles ordered when they got to her car. He grabbed her small clutch bag and fumbled for the keys. They got into the car and he pulled out the gun. He caught her staring at it. "Yeah, it's a vintage .38 special that I stole from my father's collection. Isn't it nice? A cut above the guns on the street. I wish I had time to go back and use it on him. Now you go exactly where I say and you won't get hurt."

She inserted the key into the ignition with shaky fingers. She felt a bead of sweat trickle down her neck. Her companion sat tapping his fingers against the window. She started the car.

"Drive to your bank," he ordered.

"I can only take out five hundred at a time," she said.

"Fine, then we'll go to another one after that. I need at least a grand," he said coolly.

"After I get you the money, then what?" She wanted to know what was happening.

"I'll leave you. I got a friend waiting for me, and you'll go home to sleep, *perchance to dream.*" He laughed, with a hysterical edge to his voice.

"More poetry?" she asked lightly.

"I learned it from you, Miz West. In fifth grade. You taught it to me."

"I thought I had taught you compassion and honesty," she said. "It's not too late to rethink this situation, Charles."

"Too late for that," he said.

Juliet pulled out of the parking lot. The university was surrounded by the city on two sides, a park to the west and on the east, a cemetery dating back to the Civil War. Charles pointed to the silent graves, highlighted by moonlight.

"Could be me anytime. Or it could be you," he said softly.

"We are all mortal," she said. "But it doesn't have to be soon for either one of us."

"It could be you," he said, "you're getting pretty old, aren't you?"

She looked at him impassively. She felt the old comforting rush of anger flood her senses.

As she waited for the stoplight to change, she thought she saw a red Jeep coming in her direction. She pulled out quickly and got in the way of the car. The driver blew his horn and she slammed on the brakes and skidded. Then she slowly started to drive down the quiet city street.

"What the? What's the matter with you?" Charles demanded.

"I got nervous, I thought I saw a cat on the road," she said. "I don't like to kill animals."

"Just drive," he ordered and sank back down against the seats. She drove the three miles to her bank in silence. Charles didn't speak either, he only played with the radio and tapped his foot nervously against the floor.

"How far is it? Are we going the right way?" he asked, looking out the window. "Yes, another few blocks from here. Stay calm," she said.

"I am calm. You're getting me nervous."

"You've got a gun. I don't like weapons," she said coldly.

"This is for protection and persuasion," he laughed.

She had kept looking in the rearview mirror. She thought, she hoped, she had seen a red Jeep in the distance. Or was it a mirage brought on by her overactive imagination?

"Are you going to Las Vegas tonight?" she asked, breaking the tense silence.

He held a finger up to his lips and giggled. "Shhh—it's a secret."

"Your mother and father will be worried."

"They don't give a damn about me! I cause too much trouble."

"Why did you take my class last year if you're not interested in getting an education to better yourself?" Her frayed nerves were causing her anger to swell.

"My psychiatrist thought it would be good for me. Personality development and continuing ed-u-ca-tion." He spit the word out with hostility. "Shakespeare and Mrs. West, my two favorite things on this planet."

She glared at him. "If you say so." She felt like driving the car up on the sidewalk and into a stoplight. She was tired of being controlled. But she drove on. *No use getting killed because you're mad, Juliet. You want to see your family again.*

They pulled up to the bank. The stoplight was red, red as blood, *all bedaub'd in blood.* She pinched herself above the elbow. She looked in the mirror. There was no Jeep in sight. "Another thing, Mrs. West. When this is all over, don't even think of going to the cops."

"Why not?" she asked. "Will the mafia get me?"

He laughed. "No, the vice squad. You see, I've still got the pictures and some stuff I took from your daughter's bedroom."

"What kind of stuff," she asked.

"Pink satin undies and a white lace bra and some lipstick-yeah, squeal on me and I'll say you were my lover. That could wreck your career—and your reputation."

"You took all that?" Her voice rose in shock. "So, you could destroy me if you had to? No one would believe you."

"I think they would believe me," he smirked. "You're still a hot babe. You got some wrinkles around your eyes but you're in shape. We always said that about you in school. You are one fine lady."

"How kind," she said fighting down a wave of disgust. "So now you're going to blackmail me with pictures and lingerie. How imaginative."

"I need a cover. I can say you seduced me when I was only a tender seventeen and took away my innocence. I can get you in real trouble," he sing-songed like a third grader. "Maybe jail time."

He's so angry, at himself, at life—and at me. Be careful, Juliet. He could kill you.

The light changed and she pulled up to the drive-through machine at the bank. She fumbled in her purse for her wallet.

"Hurry up," Charles commanded. "Quit playing for time."

"I'm looking for my card," she snapped. "It's dark here." As if on cue, a beam of light flooded the car and blinded her and her abductor. They sat speechless as a horn sounded loud enough to wake the dead and the entire neighborhood. Juliet had suffered enough. She pushed open her car door and unsnapped her seat belt. Charles grabbed her shoulder and she struggled, falling out of the car.

"Dammit!" she shouted, and fell sideways, hitting the blacktop with a thud. She was grateful for her ample hips as she lay there panting for breath. *I don't think I broke anything,* she thought. She waited expectantly for something to happen, lying on the ground, upside down, legs up in the air, like an overturned beetle.

She heard male voices shouting, then a gunshot filled the

night with danger and menace. The sound made her rise up in terror, fall back awkwardly and crack her skull on the ground. Then she heard a man cursing and the sounds of footsteps running away. Juliet panted, struggling to sit up, but she was in pain. Her clothes were in disarray and she felt strangled by her silver necklace. She felt impotent with rage and fear. What was happening?

"Juliet!" a familiar voice, warm and soothing, hovered near her ear, making her practically swoon with joy. "Are you all right, baby? Are you hurt?" His voice flowed over her jangled, frazzled nerves like honey. His hands gently probed her skull for injuries.

"Oh, my hip," she moaned. She opened her eyes. There he was, her Romeo.

"Sweetheart, you're a mess," he grumbled, and his fingers pulled carefully at her clothing. He picked up one of her sandals that had flown off and tenderly slipped it back on her foot. Slowly, gently he lifted her up into his arms.

"Juliet, are you hurt?" he repeated, hugging her close to his tight, hard body.

His voice snapped her into reality. He looked deep into her eyes. In the fluorescent light of the bank, he looked dark and brooding, her own special love pirate. His chiseled face studied hers intently.

"What the hell happened?" he asked, and gave her a little shake. "Did he hurt you? Speak to me."

"Jim," she said, "how did you get here? How did you know? Was that you I almost ran into? And yes," she laughed shakily, "I'm all right. Feeling stupid but all right."

"Thank God," he hugged her close. "I was frantic when I saw you."

"You saw my car by school?"

"Yes, I watched you slam on your brakes, and I noticed another person in the car." He tucked his thumbs along the inside of her collar and massaged her throat. "I was hoping to catch you before you left school but I was too late."

"How did you know I needed help?" she asked. "I could have been giving someone a ride home."

"I didn't know for sure that you needed help. I just wanted to see who was in the car and if you needed me. When I saw Charles, I guessed something wasn't right."

"You guessed correctly," she let out a sigh. "Thank you for being here."

"I'll always be here for you, Juliet, if you'll let me. We have a lot of things to talk about," he said. "I'm going to take you home. Are you well enough to drive?"

She felt her hip. It felt sore and tender. "I think I'm just going to be bruised," she said. "But tell me about the shot," she said. "What happened? You could have been killed."

"Your ex-student had at least the decency to fire the first shot straight up in the air. And then he ran. I don't know where he would have aimed if I had caught up to him," Jim said, shaking his head.

"You didn't follow him?" she asked.

"You were lying on the ground, Juliet. I had to see if you were dead or alive, I had to get to you." He pressed her to his chest. "I had to."

She shut her eyes and leaned into his strong embrace. "Thank God, you're here."

"I almost didn't come tonight. I waited for two days for you to call me. When I was in Michigan and then when I got back home but you never did. I asked you to."

She looked up into his eyes. "You told me to. That's different."

"Don't like to be ordered around by a man, do you?" He growled into her ear and pressed her harder against him. "I'm gonna have to train you to obey me once in a while, Miss teacher lady."

"Not a chance, I'm not a slave girl for a pirate," she murmured as he kissed her mouth.

"You need training and I'm going to be *your* teacher for a change," he said, kissing her again.

She closed her eyes and gave herself up to the intense sensuality of his kiss. She was floating, falling into submission when another bright light froze and illuminated the lovers and a gruff voice said, "Sorry to break this up, but what's going on?"

CHAPTER FOURTEEN

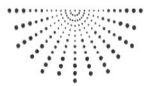

JULIET AND JIM SPRANG APART. TWO UNIFORMED POLICE OFFICERS were standing close by, looking at them like they were apparitions in the night. One was a very tall woman; the other was a man, much shorter than Juliet. *Giants and munchkins*, she thought tiredly.

"Hello," Jim said affably. "I have just been rescuing a lady," he said. "This is Mrs. West from Thomas Jefferson College. She has just been threatened by a former student and been forced at gunpoint to drive to her bank where she was supposed to get him money."

"I'm Mahoney, this is Piazza," said the taller one. "What happened, can you tell us ma'am?"

"They were interrupted by me and the kid got away," Jim answered as she stood there staring at the men in shock.

"Did he get any money?" Now the male cop was asking.

Juliet shook her head, feeling her throat closing with tears.

"You will fill out a complaint?"

"She will," Jim said, tucking her arm under his. "How did you get here so fast?"

"A neighbor reported a gunshot," Mahoney said. "So, we came as soon as we heard the call."

"I want to go home," Juliet said dully. Her head hurt and she was exhausted. "I don't want to go to the police station."

"You won't have to, ma'am," Piazza said politely. "If you would just sit here in the car, we'll take down preliminary information and we'll send a follow-up to you in the morning."

She nodded, they both got in the squad car, and she made her report. "No, I wasn't hurt, yes, I know the boy, Charles Watson, yes, I am a teacher and no, Charles doesn't have a car, at least to my knowledge." She was answering their questions plainly and without emotion. "No, he has family on the north side and yes," here she hesitated, "I think he might be suffering from a pervasive personality disorder."

"She's a teacher, with a degree in Special Education. Tell them about when he showed up at your house," Jim insisted.

"Yes, he appeared in my garage last week, and yes, I put him up for the night."

"I was a chaperone," Jim smiled. She glared.

"Yes, he took some gold jewelry belonging to my daughter."

"You didn't tell me about that," Jim said, glaring back at her.

"I didn't think it was important."

"Not important! Stealing from your house, abducting you with a gun? How about the paint on the garage door and the stuffed voodoo doll, life-sized on your deck? That's not important, either?"

The police were busy writing all this down.

"Did you fill out a report about the vandalism?" the tall woman asked.

"No," Juliet answered coldly, "I did not."

"She's too stubborn," Jim said. "And naive. She thinks problems go away with interventions."

She glared at Jim.

"Do you require medical attention, ma'am? We can call the paramedics if you need treatment."

"I am not injured," she said, "only my pride."

"If you need anything tonight, any assistance, do not hesitate to call this number." Piazza said, and gave her a card with numbers for the district station and the supervising detective.

"Thank you," she said. "I'm sure everything will be fine."

"We're going to have to arrest him, you know, ma'am, when we find him," Mahoney said. "Abduction at gunpoint is a felony."

She fought back tears. How had everything gone so wrong?

"She knows, it's okay," Jim spoke again for her. "Call us if you need us. And say hi to your dad for me," he said to Piazza. "We used to play softball together after we got out of the Marines."

"Would you like us to escort you home, ma'am?" Again, the officers were looking at her with concern.

"I'll take Mrs. West home," Jim assured them. "She'll be fine with me."

The police drove off in a hazy blur of red and blue lights. Juliet watched a lone customer drive up to the bank, near where they were standing. Jim gently squeezed her arm.

"All right? I'm going to follow you home, Juliet."

"Okay," she exhaled a deep breath, as if she had been saving it up for her entire life.

"Are you sure you're all right? I don't like how you're so pale and so cold. I was afraid you were going to faint a minute ago. That's not like you."

"I'm not used to guns and such anger," she said. "I used to think I knew all there was about human nature after being a teacher and getting divorced and raising a child, but now I think I'm all wrong. I don't know if I know anything anymore."

He took her arm. "Get in my car. I'll drive you and walk back for yours."

"No, I can do it," she protested, swatting his hand away.

He bear-hugged her and gently walked her to his car. "Come

on, Juliet, don't fight me. Do what I say, one time, it won't hurt you."

She got into the Jeep. She felt bruised, tired, and weak. Her head hurt where it had hit the pavement and her legs and shoulders were stiff and tense. She was a mess and she knew it.

He looked at her with complete understanding. "When I get you home, you're going to take a hot bath, have a drink, I'll give you a massage and then we'll sleep. And that's all we'll do, is sleep tonight. You're in pain and I'm going to comfort you."

"You don't have to do that, I'll be okay."

"Are you sure? You're not afraid? I want to check out your house and garage. I don't want to find any souvenirs from old students laying around or littering your deck."

She sighed. "You're right. I am afraid. First time ever, I think. I've been afraid for my daughter, but never for me. I feel uncomfortable, like a snake trying to shed its skin and it's stuck. I'm stuck right now and I feel foolish."

"Don't feel foolish," he said, pulling up in front of her house. "Don't be ashamed of taking a chance on people. Or a person. It shows you're human and a wonderful woman."

"I misjudged Charles," she said. They pulled up to her house.

He helped her out of the car and walked her up to the front door. He took her key and pushed open the door. He went in first.

"Don't you leave any lights on?" he complained, switching on the table lamps and the lamp on the piano.

"I thought I'd be home before dark," she said.

"Stay here," he commanded. He checked each bedroom, the bathroom, went into the kitchen and then she heard him out on the deck. He came back to her where she stood idly playing a few chords on the piano. "Lock the back door after me."

She stared at him and continued to play. He walked over to her and took her hands off the keys. "You will have to give me a concert later. I can't wait to hear you play," he said, and took her arm. "But now I want you to come with me, Juliet, and lock the door while I go check around back."

She laughed softly, played another two chords and then stopped. *"Oh shut the door and when thou hast done so, come weep with me, past hope, past cure, past help.* How appropriate," she murmured, and followed him meekly into the kitchen.

"Do you have to have a quote for everything?" he asked.

"Since I met you, Jimmy, everything has happened to me. It's like being in the middle of one big epic poem," she said, feeling her humor slowly returning.

"Right, and this is Beowulf or Star Wars," he finished with a smile.

"Something like that," she said and locked the door.

She put the kettle on for a cup of tea. She felt tired but so keyed up that she was ready to snap. She thought about the weekend. Her date with Jim, finding Charles in her house, and now this frightening abduction—what next? She pinched her arm angrily. This was not the first time she had made a mistake about a man. First it had been with Tony, her ex-husband. Then an artist she had dated after her divorce. He had wanted fun with no commitment, and she had been shocked at how shallow a forty-year-old man could be. And now with James—how could she really tell what was in his heart?

She heard a knock at the back door. "Juliet, let me in, please?"

She opened the door. "Any demons about? Any ghosts or goblins or stuffed dummies?" she asked him with a sad smile.

"I'm the only dummy around here," he said, and watched her as she poured boiling water in a china teapot and added loose tea leaves.

"Smells good," he said.

"It's Chinese tea, pale green and soothing," she said. "Will you join me?"

"Yes, I'll join you," he said. He walked over to her and put his hands on her shoulders. "Got any brandy or whiskey around here?"

"In the living room, in the bar, remember?" she asked him. "Would you like a drink?"

"Not really, but I'd say you do," he said. "You're as white as a ghost. You're in shock. I want you to take a hot bath and have a sip of brandy with your tea. You don't look good, darling."

"Sorry, I'm so scary looking," she said lightly, feeling the tears that she had holding back for an hour moistening her eyes.

"You're beautiful, gorgeous, you're my goddess, voluptuous and desirable," he said, pulling her against him. "But you're pale and sad and look like you're about ready to be laid in your sepulcher or tomb or whatever they call it," he said, hugging her tenderly. "You had a fright tonight, Juliet. Go ahead, admit it, don't be so tough all the time."

She pushed him gently away. "I've had to be tough. I supported a man and a daughter for years and now I'm trying to gracefully take care of myself. I have to be tough," she repeated with a stubborn look.

"All right, okay, you're an Amazon, you're Wonder Woman," he said. "But tonight, just one time," he told her, "you're going to relax."

He walked off into the living room and she poured tea. *Relax? Sure, why not?* She waited for him a minute, sipping scalding hot tea that flooded her nose with steam and its pungent aroma.

"Jim?" she called out. No answer. She got up to look. There was a bottle of brandy open on the bar and the stereo was playing Ella Fitzgerald. Her luscious voice wrapped around the lyrics to 'I Love Paris.' Instant tranquility and sensuality. She felt warm. "James, where are you?"

"Right here, I'm in the bathroom," he answered. "Come on in."

"More orders?" she asked. "Must you always be so bossy?" She walked into the bathroom and caught her breath. He was standing over a tub full of steaming water filled with bubbles.

The jasmine bubble bath that had been a gift from her granddaughter, last Christmas.

"Must you always be so argumentative?" he asked with a boyish grin. He was wearing a *Semper Fi* t-shirt and looked about twenty years old. She pinched herself over the right elbow. *This must be a dream*, she thought.

"Now quit pinching yourself and acting psycho," he told her, taking her gently by the arm. In her hand he placed a small glass of brandy. Its amber color fascinated her and she stared at it intently. "What's the matter with you?" he demanded. "Have you gone a little crazy tonight?"

"Yes, very crazy," she giggled. She leaned over the bathtub and inhaled the sweet aroma. "What's all this?" she asked. *"Double, double toil and trouble, cauldron bum and fire bubble,"* she intoned. "See? I've become a crazy witch." She took a small sip of brandy and started to cough. He grabbed the glass and gently stroked her back.

"Careful," he said. "I want to put a little color in your cheeks, not have you fall into a hacking fit—or start quoting Macbeth," he added with a wicked look at her.

"Mr. Sanders, I apologize," she said grandly as he started unbuttoning her skirt, "I wronged you. You are much more refined than any Marine I have ever met. And what?" here she tried slapping his hand away, "are you doing?"

"Thank you for the compliment, dear lady, but I am trying to get you take a warm bath and to do that," here he slapped her hands away gently, "I am going to have to take off your clothes unless you can cooperate for one minute and do it yourself."

She stared in awe at his handsome golden beauty. How lucky to be rescued by such a hunk. She kept staring. "Well, can you?" he asked, hands on hips.

She wanted to kiss the cleft in his tanned chin.

"Can I do what?" she asked.

"Take off your clothes," he asked gently.

"Take off my clothes?" she asked.

"You are going to take a bubble bath," he explained patiently, as if to a five-year-old.

"I am?" she inquired politely. "No wait!" she said. "I can do this myself."

"Then do it," he said. "I'll come back in two minutes with our tea, and lady, you had better be in this bathtub—or else."

CHAPTER FIFTEEN

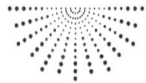

WHO DOES HE THINK HE IS? SHE THOUGHT, STRUGGLING OUT OF HER clothes and shoes. She took a tiny sip of brandy and coughed. Grimacing, she unhooked her bra and stepped out of lace hi-cut panties.

She eased into the bathtub and gasped. The warm water caressed every frazzled and frightened nerve in her body. She felt her bruised hip responding to the warmth. Jim walked in as she had her hands in her hair, rubbing the sore spot on the back of her head.

Juliet sunk down beneath the bubbles. She felt his intense scrutiny and flushed.

"How am I doing?" she asked with a scowl.

"What's up with your head?" he demanded.

"You ask too many questions," she said. He immediately dropped down beside her. His strong hands felt her skull, circling gently until he felt the bump in question.

"Hey, what's this?" he demanded. "You didn't tell me about this."

"It's okay, it's nothing, just a little bump," she said.

"Just a little bump?" he said with a frown. "Lady, I've seen bumps smaller than this in the Marines that caused concussions. Damn, I don't like this," he frowned and leaned over her. His body, muscled and golden brown, exuded his personal scent— lemons, masculine sweat, now infused with tea and brandy.

"I'm fine," she insisted, trying not to gasp at his aroma. "All my family have very hard heads."

"The Wests?" he took a sip of his brandy and watched her closely.

"I'm not a West, that's my ex-husband's name. I'm Italian, we're Carlucci's and we have very hard heads and very thick skins," she explained. "So that's why I'm not afraid."

"And that's why you're such a stubborn little girl," he said, picking up a pink sponge. He made soft, swirling movements around her neck and shoulders that made her skin tingle. "You can't tell an Italian anything," he complained.

"What do you mean by that?" she asked. "What do you know about Italians?"

"One of my best buddies in the Marines was Italian, and I work with Italian stone and marble cutters, they think they're Michelangelo and they do great work and now after knowing you lady, I can see you're all Capulet, all beautiful and one big pain in the neck," he finished plunging the sponge beneath the water's surface to caress her back and buttocks.

She gasped again and pushed his hand away. "Please!" she said. "I'm trying to relax."

"Who said you were?" he asked with a grin.

"You did," she said.

"And you're not relaxing?"

"If you could only behave for a little while then maybe I could," she explained. "But when you're near me and when you keep touching me like that, it's hard to stay calm."

"Like what?" he asked. "Like this?" He roved his hands through the warm soapy water, touching her breasts, her thighs and her sore hip.

"Yes," she sighed again. "Please, stop it. I can't think straight when you do that."

He looked a little ashamed of himself. "Sorry, I know you've been through hell just now, but I can't help myself. You look so pretty and I was so worried about you tonight. And why didn't you call me when I was gone?"

"I was raised back with Abraham Lincoln," she said, "young ladies were taught not to call men, but to wait for their call. Surely you might have heard of that?"

"Oh, I get it, Annette Funicello and Sandra Dee, Doris Day and Sex and the Single Girl. You're a real old-fashioned kind of girl, aren't you, Juliet? No sex without marriage, no love without commitment."

"I don't know about that," she said, looking him straight in the eye, "last week I took a real chance on both."

"Yes, you did," he said, and handed her the glass of brandy. "Sip, please, be a good girl for me. And I'll be right back."

She closed her eyes. A good girl? He talked to her like she was in high school. Her tense muscles were starting to relax. Maybe it would be nice to live with a man. A real supportive man for once in her life. She wondered. She was involved in a literary fantasy of pirates and rose-throwing fifteenth century noblemen when she felt a cold lump against the back of her skull.

"Oh, my goodness," she gasped, as the ice pack found the sensitive spot. "This is truly horrendous."

"Are you all right, little girl?" She opened her eyes and was dazzled by the sea blue light of his eyes. "You need some aspirin or whatever this stuff is." He shook out a little blue pill from a plastic bottle. "Non-aspirin pain reliever," he read. "Use these much?"

"Just when I get an attack of being an old, arthritic woman," she said mercilessly.

"Ouch," he said. "You don't look that old to me, grandmaw," he leered at her. "Here, take this," he said, and put the pill on her tongue. He handed her a glass of water and she obediently swallowed the pill.

"The color of your eyes," she mumbled incoherently.

"What's the color of my eyes?" he asked.

"The pill, it was the same pretty, intense blue," she said seriously.

"Right, of course it was," he said, and started to massage her shoulders.

"Ooooh," she sighed. "I am so stiff and sore. What a night. What a fool I am."

"Don't be so hard on yourself," he said as his hands rubbed semi-circles along her shoulders. "Here, turn on your side." She moved over a little and his hands continued a roving tour of her back, legs and hips. "You took a chance on somebody and they didn't pan out. At least you took a chance. At least you believe in the power of people and change. Don't be ashamed of that."

"A few days ago you were telling me that I was crazy to believe in a person who had issues," she grumbled. "You didn't trust Charles at all."

"I know, I know," he said. "I was skeptical at first," he said, taking the sponge and wringing warm waterfalls of water over her flesh. "But then I said, hey, Juliet is a teacher, she knows kids, she knows people. She's experienced with psychology."

"I thought I was," she said, shaking her head. "But I seem to have been wrong. I got burned, didn't I?"

"You're not the only one who's been burned," he said. "I've lent money to my workers a lot of times and even though most have paid me back and on time, there's been a couple who haven't and then cussed me out when I asked them what the trouble was. You're not the only one who has been wrong."

"Thank you for saying that," she said, squirming a little as his hands dripped water over her bosom, "I appreciate it."

"Are you all right?" he asked, all concern. "Is the water too hot? Have I burned you?"

147

"Only with the warmth of your concern," she said, staring at her pink toenails that were sticking out amid the bubbles. She also observed one of the tips of her breasts was peeking through the suds and she sunk down lower into the bathtub.

"Look at me, Juliet," he said, observing her modest blush.

"Why?" she asked, still staring at her toes. "I can hear you perfectly."

"Juliet," he said in a low voice. "Look at me."

"Still bossy as ever," she grumbled, and looked up annoyed at his command. The loving look in his eyes almost blew her out of the water. She stared, mesmerized by his beautiful face.

"Did you think you would turn to stone like that Medusa you were talking about in class last week?" he demanded with a sexy smile.

"Something like that," she admitted, "and right now I feel like I've got a head full of writhing snakes. Although when I'm looking at you, I'm not a piece of stone. I'm on fire."

"I like that, Juliet, I like it that you feel warm when you look at me, I like that very much," he said, looking deep into her eyes. He brushed a stray bubble off her chin and smiled. "But listen up, girlfriend. I want to tell you something."

"Yes?" she said, and felt her insides getting all soft and nervous at his serious tone.

"You know," he said softly, "how I feel about you."

"Yes, I know. I mean, I think I know," she said.

"If you think that anything has changed from last week to this one, you are wrong, Miss teacher lady. I'm in love with you and I want to be with you. This feels all too right to be wrong."

She looked at him and exhaled a deep breath.

"Thank you for saying that, but you go too fast," she said. "You must believe that I do care for you, I'm immensely attracted to you, but I was married for twenty-five years," she said forcefully. "Twenty-five years," she repeated, hitting her knee with her fist. "And I've been alone now for five years and I don't know what I feel anymore. I don't know what I want. Surely you can understand that?"

"I can understand that," he said. "But I wanted you to know how I feel. You are very important to me. And," he added with a wry look, "we're not gonna make love tonight."

Her eyes opened, way, way open.

"We're not?" she asked. "All this back rubbing and brandy was just for my health?" she asked in a voice that rose with indignation.

"Miss Juliet, I still say you've got a dirty mind," he sighed. "It must come from reading too much lit-er-a-ture," he stretched it out with a wicked grin. "Yes, I am concerned about you," he said. "And I'm not gonna make love to you, as much as I'm dying to, when you've got a golf ball on the back of your head and you've been kidnapped tonight by a lunatic. Okay?" He stood up and grabbed her bathrobe. "I wanted you to know this before I get you out of the tub. You are perfectly safe with me, Juliet. I'm going to hold you and kiss you a little and make sure you don't have a headache. We're going to sleep like babies together." He picked up the robe and held it up over her. "Do you need help?"

"No, I can do it," she said, and rose up out of the warm water. She shivered for a split second as the cool air hit her heated flesh. He wrapped her in a luxurious pink terry cloth robe and helped her out of the tub. "Thank you, you are too sweet," she said.

"My pleasure," he replied. "Come on, let's get you into bed."

She sat tiredly on the edge of the bed. He had turned on the air conditioner and cool gusts of air were filling the room. He handed her the chaste pink and white nightgown.

"Do you need help with this?" he asked her.

"No," she said, "I think I can just about manage to put on my own nightgown, battered and bruised as I am."

"Hey, don't get down now," he said, putting his hand under her chin. "Don't get depressed."

Tears filled her eyes. She felt like she was going to pieces.

"I'm trying not to," she whispered. "I guess it has been a shock, after all."

"Of course, it has," he said. "Here, let me." He gently slipped the robe off her body, and put the sweet old granny nightgown over her head. She tugged it down quickly.

"I must look like hell," she said, running her hands through her tousled, wet hair.

"You look like an angel," he said, and carefully lifted her legs and put them on the bed. He placed a stack of pillows behind her head and positioned the ice pack on her sore spot. On the nightstand next to the bed, he placed her cup of tea and small glass of brandy.

"This is lovely service," she said. "Thank you for taking such good care of me."

"My pleasure," he said, and gently kissed her lips. His kiss was sweet from the brandy and salty from a bit of sweat induced by the night's excitement.

"*You kiss by the book,*" she quoted, and he smiled. She sighed and sank down among the pillows. "Aren't you going to join me?" she asked him.

"After a shower," he said, pulling off his shirt. "If you don't mind, that is."

"No, please," she said, staring at his tanned, rock hard body. "Be my guest. You must be hot and tired, too." She kept staring. His chest muscles were well-defined halfmoons and his stomach sported that valued six-pack of muscles that men and women at gyms worked for years to obtain. His torso was covered with a light sprinkling of golden hair that enhanced his masculine beauty. His waist was lean and taut, and his jeans clung to his hips provocatively. She was entranced by his healthy good-looks and by the sweet smile that hung on his lips.

"You are so beautiful," she said.

He smiled and hung his head. "Shucks, ma'am, that's no way

to talk to a old dude like me. You'll turn my head and then I'll never be able to dig a sewer again."

"That's okay," she smiled, "you can be a movie star or an artist's model or something where you don't have to hide in a sewer. It would be a waste hiding that physique. You look like a Greek statue."

"Gosh, I'm blushing," he said. "Miss teacher lady, you really know how to give a guy a compliment. I've never been called a statue before."

She reached up and traced her fingers along his hard stomach and chest. She brushed her fingertips lightly along the gilded streak of hairs below his navel. He shivered and stopped her hand from further wanderings.

"Enough, Lady Juliet, I must away," he laughed. "You are sending all my good intentions about the evening whistling down the wind."

"What does that mean?" she asked, taking his lean hand and rubbing it against her cheek.

"It means if I'm not going to make love to you, I'd better take that shower right away." he said. "And make it pretty damn cold."

He kissed her swiftly on the mouth and then made a fast getaway into the bathroom before she could grab him for more kisses. She heard him singing the old Doors tune, *Come on Baby Light my Fire*, before he turned the shower on full blast and changed to the *Halls of Montezuma*, the Marine Corps song. Well, he had certainly lit her fire, all right. She stretched from her toes to her stiff neck and sighed.

She turned on the TV and surfed through all her favorite movie channels. As if on cue, there appeared the face of Leonardo DiCaprio, a swimming Romeo, coaxing a modem Juliet to come out and play. The 90's version of her beloved romance was heavy into guns and violence, gangs and adults who acted without a thought for consequences. She shivered and pulled the sheet up under her neck.

The bathroom door opened and Jim walked in the room. She smiled at him. He looked so young and vulnerable, wrapped in one of her pink bath sheets. Little beads of water clung to his spiky blond hair. He wore a tiny gold cross around his neck. He saw her looking at the cross.

"It belonged to my mother," he said. "She's gone, too. The year after Barbara. All my favorite ladies have left me. Can you wonder that I've been on the road looking for babes and culture and cheap thrills?" he asked, leaning over her on the bed. He looked dangerous and seductive and for once she was not afraid to look deep into his eyes.

"Where do I fit in?" she asked him with a pout on her full lips. "Am I the culture, one of the babes, or the cheap thrill?"

He looked down at her and his face was unfathomable with unknown emotion.

"You're all three to me, Juliet," he murmured, and covered her body with his own. His lips were warm and tender, and as she listened to an updated version of her favorite play in the background, she surrendered to the fulfillment of his kiss. Everything that had happened to her since she had met him was only an exciting prelude to the reality of being in his arms. She was thirteen and a Juliet, he was her young, dashing Romeo. His lips released hers for an instant and she sighed. She felt her breath gently fanning back to her from his adoring face.

"Ah, Juliet, you're so sweet," he said. "And what's this?" he turned and frowned at the TV. "Hey, I've watched this with my kids, it's way too brutal for a tender poet like me," he said, and grabbed the remote and turned it off.

"I like that movie, even though it's rough," she said. "It's powerful." She covered his face with a blast of little kisses. "You're powerful."

"I hope I am," he said, and silenced her with one swift, deep kiss that lifted her right off the mattress with its intensity. He kissed her with a mastery she had only experienced in dreams.

Through the towel she could feel every sinew and muscle in his fabulous body and when she rubbed her hands up and down his hard, chiseled back he moaned and buried his lips in the small of her neck. "Juliet," he sighed. When she tried to put her hand gently under the pink towel to massage his enormous manhood, he lifted his head and pushed her hand away.

"Enough," he said. "We will be good tonight."

She looked up at him with love-darkened eyes and swollen lips.

"Why tonight? Why be good, especially after everything we've been through? Why not make love to me, Jimmy, I won't be mad at you in the morning, I swear I won't, I swear it," she said in a shaky voice.

"*Oh, swear not at all*," he said, equally emotional. "I mean it, Juliet, tonight we're just going to be close." He jumped up from the bed and left her feeling lost, confused and throbbing.

"Show me where to find some shorts," he said and she wordlessly pointed to the bottom drawer of her dresser. He pulled on a pair of navy blue running shorts He looked like a college boy, clean-cut and healthy. She watched him warily.

"What now?" she asked. "Should we read poetry together?"

"Something like that," he grinned. He got back into bed with her, carefully arranged his long frame against hers, and covered them with the cool sheet. She turned a sad face up to meet his. "Hey, don't look at me like that. Don't be sad. I'm only doing this for your own good, young lady."

"I'm not so young or so good," she said, making a face at him. "I'm over twenty-one."

"I noticed," he said and flicked the tip of her nose. "But you don't understand me, Juliet, you don't know me well enough. With ladies I love, I don't play."

"How do you mean?" she asked. He switched off the light and turned on the small stained-glass night light.

"A lot has happened since we met, I know it. We haven't had a lot of time just to talk about ourselves and what we like about life," he said. "I know I've been rushing you, but that's me," he smiled at her. "I'm a maniac, and when I see somebody I like, I mean love, I just can't wait."

"You keep saying love," she said. "How can you know you love me in only three weeks?"

"I know," he said. "I have instincts."

She watched his face in the semi-darkness. "You look so sincere and serious."

"I am serious about you," he said. "Please think about this. I love you, Juliet, and I want to be in a relationship with you."

"How can you talk about relationships?" she demanded. "We've only known each other for such a short time. I was married for twenty-five years, James, remember? I am not sure I know how to be in a new relationship, anymore."

"I remember. But I know that when something's right, it's right. And this is only the second time in my life that I've got this feeling of—perfection, no—total happiness. And besides, you let me make love to you. You asked me to. Remember?"

"I know," she said. "How could I forget? You're only the second man that I've slept with in thirty years."

"You see? Don't you think that means something?" he asked her.

"I don't know what came over me that night," she said. "It must have been the fear, the shock of being mugged or whatever you want to call it."

"It was love," he said. "Can't you see that?" He paused and stared at her. "Listen, were you going to make love with me the night we went out dancing and we found Charles in your garage?"

"Yes," she admitted slowly, "at least I thought we were."

"Then what happened after that? What made you stop trusting me?"

Juliet moaned in exasperation and frustration at his

unattainable nearness. "Are you my analyst now?" she asked, raising up on one elbow to frown at him. "I thought you were trying to be my lover."

"No, you're wrong," he said. "I'm trying to be your husband."

"Husband? Wow. I don't know what to say," she said, sinking back onto the pillows in confusion. Her face was burning with pleasure. "I was wrong about Charles and—"

"And you think that you're wrong about me?" he loomed above her in the semi-darkness.

"My mistake about Charles made me wonder if I had rushed into a relationship with you without thinking things through. What do I really feel about you? And where do I want things to go?"

"Lady, you do a lot of thinking," he said, rolling over and staring up at the ceiling. "Don't you ever do any feeling?"

"Of course, I do," she protested. "That's not fair."

"It's not? You mean you don't write every man you meet down in a grade book?"

"That's an interesting idea," she said. "Maybe I should start."

"You know, put us all down in one of those funky green books with those thousand little squares and lines like my fifth grade teacher, Miss Stoker, used to carry with her. If you ever got out of line, out came the book and BAM! a check mark. If you were really bad then you got a red check mark and if you were—"

"A troublemaker?" she couldn't resist.

"A double red check mark. My mom gave her a box of red pens for Christmas that year," he chuckled.

"That's a fascinating story." She gently placed her hand on his flat abdomen and put her cheek against his shoulder. "You don't mind if I cuddle up next to you, do you Romeo?"

"No," he said softly. "You feel great, Lady Juliet."

They lay in companionable silence for a minute. She heard the ticking of the clock, felt the beating of her heart, smelled his citrus cologne and the fabulous male scent that was enveloping her. She was in a cocoon of protection. The bed would hold and protect her until she pushed her way out, at last, she hoped, a beautiful butterfly, secure in his love. She sighed.

"Feeling better?" he asked.

"A little," she said. "I'm sorry I'm being so temperamental."

"That's okay," he said, snuggling his chin on the top of her head. "But tell me, Miss teacher lady, what grade would you give me?"

"In what?"

"Oh, the whole report card," he said. "How about intelligence?"

"An A," she said. "You're very smart."

"How about attendance?"

"B-plus" she said. "You missed a class, remember? I believe you had a date with a lady."

"Forget that nonsense," he groaned. "How about attitude?"

"Now that's a C-minus because you've been so fresh and smart-mouthed during class. Always trying to score a joke off the teacher," she said disapprovingly.

"And a lover?" he asked softly.

"A-minus," she said without hesitation.

"Why the minus?" he asked. "How can I improve?"

"You won't kiss me again tonight," she said. "That's why."

"I'll give you more when you're fully recovered," he promised.

"And you'll make love to me?" she queried.

He put her hands against his lips, encircled her waist with a strong arm and looked deeply into her eyes.

"I'll make love to you again when you promise to marry me, Juliet."

CHAPTER SIXTEEN

SLEEP WAS ELUSIVE. LONG AFTER JIM HAD DROPPED HIS BOMBSHELL and had fallen asleep with her cradled gently in his arms, she had looked up at the ceiling, watching the fan slowly turning. *He loves me, he loves me not,* she thought with each complete spin. *How about, I love him, I love him not?* She was turning and spinning in a chasm of thought. So much had happened so fast. Love, fear, and the termination of her five-year celibacy—longer if you counted the very cold and barren final years of her marriage. And now a wealth of warmth and admiration from a gorgeous pirate Romeo who wanted to marry her.

She stared up and up for hours. There was a crescent moon outside her window, floating in the inky sky. She could not let her fears ruin her chance of happiness. This might be the last chance. *Then, I defy you, stars,* she thought and finally drifted off to sleep, reveling in his strong arms around her.

She heard in her subconscious the church bells strike one, then two, and she was dreaming. She was running through the streets of Verona wearing a flowing white gown, encrusted with seed pearls and diamonds that formed the shapes of stars and roses. She could not find the church in which she was going to be married.

She ran recklessly through the ancient, cobbled streets, hearing an organ play the traditional Wedding March. *It hasn't been written yet*, she thought. This is the wrong century, two hundred and fifty years too soon, and pinched herself above the elbow.

She kept running past balconies and stone castles. As she flew by a tavern, a pirate stuck out his gnarled arm and tried to grab her hand. She shrieked and pushed him away but noticed a rose and star tattoo on his right bicep. The street turned to sand and she began to sink through the ground.

"Help me, help me," she called out and she felt the hands of angels pulling her upwards. When she arose out of the sand, she was standing up high on a silver pedestal wearing only one glass slipper. The pedestal was covered with mirrors and when she looked down beneath her feet, she saw that she was an old woman with white hair and a face full of grooves and wrinkles. *I'm the Grand Canyon*, she thought, *I'm so old*, and began to pull off the white dress, shedding layers and layers of silk and tulle, like a snake shedding designer skin.

She woke up, totally wrapped in the sheets like a mummy. She had been sweating in fear and put a hand up to her damp forehead.

"My God," she whispered, "what a dream. I'm going crazy. I need a therapist or a vacation." Her companion, her Romeo, was no longer sharing her bed. She pushed the tangled sheets away in exasperation. She put on her robe and refused to look in the mirror. *I'll scare him. Let him see the real me.*

Once again, the sound of voices and laughter and the smell of coffee assailed her senses as she walked through her house. Deja vu. The breakfast club had again assembled in her kitchen. Jim was cooking eggs while Lois and Beatrice sipped coffee and eyed him appreciatively. He had put on her Lady Macbeth t-shirt and the face of the mad woman stared back at her from his broad chest.

"I hope I don't look as bad as she does," Juliet said, looking at Jim's shirt.

"You look as beautiful as ever," Jim said and kissed her cheek. "Good morning, baby."

"Good morning," she croaked out to them. "My throat is so dry."

"Have some juice," Lois said, and poured her a glass.

Juliet took a healthy swallow. "Thank you," she said. "I was parched and I just had the weirdest dream."

"We hear you had the weirdest night," Beatrice said, wide-eyed with concern. "I can't believe you were kidnapped."

Juliet patted the young woman's hand.

"I wasn't really kidnapped. I was just forcefully persuaded to go in search of cash."

"Horrible boy," Lois said. "The nerve of him after you taught him when he was a kid. I don't care what you say, Juliet, but he deserves to be prosecuted. He's really a criminal."

"I—I suppose so," Juliet hesitated. Jim placed plates of steaming scrambled eggs in front of the women.

"Enjoy, ladies," he said. He sat down next to Juliet. "You listen to Lois," he said to her, "she knows what she's saying. Enough of this fooling around, Juliet. This is not a scene from one of your plays. This is reality."

"Yes, sir," she sighed. "I suppose you're right. I suppose Charles will be found eventually," she said, sprinkling salt and pepper on her eggs. "But I hope not for a while."

"Sorry, honey, but he was picked up last night," Lois told her. "After you eat your breakfast, dearest, we're going downtown so you can identify him."

"I am?" Juliet's heart was slamming uncomfortably against her chest.

"You've got to," Beatrice said. "He's dangerous."

"She's right," Jim said. "You can't get him off this time with your kindness." He placed a tender hand on her shoulder and she felt her eyes prick with tears.

"What will he be charged with?" she asked Lois.

"Probably unlawful use and possession of a firearm, extortion or robbery, possibly abduction and whatever unfinished business he had with drug dealers and loan sharks," she said.

Juliet put down her fork. "But that means he'll have to go to jail. Possibly for years!"

"He broke the law," Lois said. "Many of them. And you could have been hurt."

"She's right," Jim agreed. "This situation is bigger than your kindness, Juliet. Now you have to follow the law."

"I know," she sighed. "But I feel terrible. I made a mistake about Charles. I thought he was interested in literature and in turning his life around. He told me once he was interested in acting. I thought my classes could help him. I guess he was only interested in what I could do for him."

"You took a chance," Lois said. "A great big chance. No one can blame you for wanting to help a kid out."

"You're wonderful," Beatrice said. "And so brave."

"She is wonderful," Jim said. "Eat your eggs, Juliet."

"Yes, Dad," she said and obediently took another mouthful.

"You've done wonders with her," Lois said to Jim. "She seems so much less ornery and even does what she's told, once in a while."

"Yes, Juliet is an excellent student," Jim agreed. Juliet stuck her tongue out at them both.

Beatrice laughed. "You guys are so much fun," she said.

"We're a riot," Juliet said. "Absolute nuts."

Lois stood up. "Finish your breakfast, dear one. I'll come back in twenty minutes and take you downtown."

"This morning?" Juliet said in surprise.

"They can't hold him forever without charging him," Lois said firmly. "You have to identify Charles."

"So, they can put him away?" Juliet said, shaking her head unhappily.

"So that he can start to get help," Lois said.

"In jail?" Juliet said in disbelief.

"There are rehab programs and counselors even in jail," Jim said. "Charles needs more help than even you gave him. You have to believe that."

"I know," she said. "It just seems so sad." She sighed and put down her coffee cup. "Okay, Lois, I'll be ready. Thanks for coming over to check on me, both of you." Beatrice threw her arms around Juliet. "I'm glad you're safe," she said.

After the women left, Juliet sat idly playing with a piece of toast. She watched Jim washing dishes at the sink, looking very domestic and very much a part of her life.

"So, what was last night all about?" she said at last. "Were you trying to teach me a lesson?"

"Not a lesson," he said, turning off the faucets. He picked up a dishtowel and expertly dried a frying pan before he spoke again. "I was serious, Juliet. I meant everything I said last night. And everything I did."

"You mean everything you didn't do," she said with a wry smile. "I believe you put the brakes on our affair."

"Yeah, 'cause I don't want an affair," he said. He sat down next to her and placed his fingers under her trembling chin. "You know that I won't sleep with you again until you agree to marry me," he said. "Let's get that clear. I'll date you and take you out until the end of time, but no sex. I want our relationship to be special."

"This is crazy," she said. "This is like some weird reverse emotional game. Aren't we too old for games?"

"This is not a game," he answered her, "it's like an insurance policy to protect our love. I'm gonna make you take us seriously. I'm not throwing away our future because we gave in one night to our emotions."

"This is not the man I met in class three weeks ago," she said.

"First impressions are deceiving," he said. "Didn't you say you weren't the best judge of character?"

"You can't compare a student with a lover," she said.

"No? We're all people. You think that because you were wrong about Charles you are wrong about me, don't you? Well, I'm going to prove to you that you are a wonderful woman who believes in the power of love, Juliet." He took her hand and massaged her fingers gently. "How's your head feeling this morning?"

"I have the headache from hell," she said.

"I'm sure you do and it's not helping your mood," he said. "So, listen up, my love. We had a blissful preview of paradise last week, you and me, and now it's time to plan the rest of our lives together."

"Prologue becomes Act One?" she asked with a little smile.

"Yes, and Act Two and Three until we're old and grey, darling."

"You may not have noticed this," she said, making a face at him, "but I am old and grey. Except I cover it up," she said, touching her streaked, highlighted hair.

"I have noticed that you're beautiful, intelligent, a loving mother and grandmother, and one hell of a teacher and lover. And I love you," he said, kissing her hand.

She pulled her fingers away, feeling an electric shock from the warmth of his lips.

"Stop it, behave yourself!" she protested. "When you touch me, I can't think."

"Lady, I know the feeling," he agreed. "So, what do you think about my proposition? I mean, my proposal," he grinned.

"I admit things have been a little unconventional between us," she said.

"You could say that," he agreed.

"We didn't have a chance to have a regular relationship," she continued.

"Yeah, but I wasn't the one with paint on my garage door and stuffed dolls on my deck and young men lurking in every dark corner now, was I?"

She grew warm at his scrutiny. "I know," she sighed. "It's all my fault, isn't it? If I hadn't had all this intrigue in my life then we could have gone out on a regular date and let things develop naturally. We could have gotten to know each other more conventionally. Although," she said with a wicked look, "as I remember, a certain person started calling me up inquiring about buds of love, and babes, and showed up in my alley uninvited."

"I was afraid of you," he admitted. "I thought she's so classy and beautiful if I ask her out to dinner she'll just laugh in my face. I'm too uncouth and rough for a lady like you," he said. "So, I got crazy and aggressive and tried to make you like me."

"Well, it worked," she said. "It worked just fine. See what kind of mess you've gotten us in?"

"I like this kind of mess," he said and kissed her lips.

Juliet closed her eyes and surrendered to his kiss. She could almost breathe in his love and enthusiasm. For a minute his tongue darted inside her mouth and explored hers with a gentleness that made her woozy. She put her hands around his neck and he pressed her close to him. She was his, totally. All he had to do was walk her back to bed and she would be his.

He finally released her mouth, disentangled their bodies and she moaned.

"I'm dizzy," she complained gently. "You're a fabulous kisser."

"You're tired," he said, smiling down at her. "You need to take a shower and get dressed. Lois is waiting for you. Sweetheart, we're through smooching for a while. Come with me," he said and walked her to the bathroom. "Do you need help?"

"If you come in here with me, you're going to be in trouble," she said.

"You'll molest me and take advantage of me?" he asked with a grin.

"I'm about ready to throw you over my shoulder and carry you off to the cave," she said.

He laughed delightedly. "That's good, babe. That means that you're weakening. Soon I'll have you on my side." The sound of his laughter filled her ears for hours after he was gone.

Lois picked her up as promised and drove her to the police station. "Just stay calm," her friend ordered. "He won't have to see you at all. You'll pick him out of the line-up, sign a paper, and that's it."

"Won't I have to go to court?" she asked.

"Probably not, because he has some other outstanding warrant, drugs and extortion, since he turned eighteen."

"He does? How could someone so young go so wrong?"

Lois patted her hand. "He had a troubled childhood and some psychological issues that were never fully addressed. He's got problems."

She picked out Charles from the line-up. He was standing there looking bored, putting on a show of looking cool and defiant. He did not look scared and Juliet felt so bad for his family and for him.

"All right?" Lois asked, after Juliet had signed the papers and they had gone outside.

"I'll be okay," she said. "I'm getting used to the idea that I was wrong."

"It's not easy, is it?" Lois agreed. "Want to go get coffee?"

"Thanks, but I want to go home," Juliet said. "I have work to do before class tonight."

"Why don't you cancel class?" Lois asked. "You must be exhausted."

"I don't want to cancel. I might not be able to reach all the students in time and I don't want to disappoint anyone."

"Always the great teacher," Lois said. "You amaze me, Juliet. You are so strong."

Juliet didn't feel strong when she went to the studio that morning. Her legs felt weak like spaghetti and her arm muscles were tight and stiff. She made herself stretch and walk on a treadmill for a while, just to feel like she was part of the human race again. She bought a huge iced tea from the cafe and walked slowly home, thinking about her life.

If she told him yes, I will marry you, then what? Would they set a date and then fall into bed? What if this was a double ploy on his part? He would play hard to get to make her want him even more. Maybe he didn't want to get married at all. Maybe he was counting on her to refuse.

Then why not make love to me, she thought. It would all be so easy the other way. Now there's the future hanging over our heads.

Juliet walked down the alley behind her house. It was quiet and peaceful. Along fences grew morning glories and wildflowers. There were some interesting pieces of old furniture next to the dumpsters and she fondly remember how she used to drag home chairs in the early days of her marriage and would paint and recover them. They hadn't much money in the early days, she and Tony. She had worked hard to make a nice home for them.

She walked through the back gate and pinched herself above the elbow. As if her mind had conjured him up, there sat Tony on her deck, reading the sports page and drinking a cup of coffee. *How cozy,* she thought, *how bizarre.*

"I was just thinking about you," she said, slowly walking up the stairs. "And here you are."

"I hope they were good thoughts, Juliet," he said, getting up to greet her.

"Just thoughts from the past, how I used to take chairs in from the alley and fix them up," she said.

"I remember the year we sat on chairs covered with fake zebra fur and painted purple," he smiled.

"My punk year," she said. "And they were cheap."

He frowned a little. Tony didn't like to be reminded about not having money.

"We could have used my mother's dining room set, but you wouldn't hear of it," he said.

"It was more fun being creative," she explained. "But surely you didn't come over here to talk about furniture?"

"No, Karen and I heard about your attack last night, and I wanted to see if you were all right," he explained.

"Bad news travels fast," she said lightly.

"Our neighbor's son works at the police station where they picked up the boy," he said. "I didn't know if I should call Colette or if you needed help here."

"Don't call our daughter," she said, "let her finish her vacation in peace. There's nothing she can do. It's all over anyway."

Her ex-husband looked at her. He was about her height and his hair was thinning a bit on top. He had added a few pounds around the middle and usually had a half-serious, half-worried expression on his face. Today was no different. He looked at her a little nervously and then cleared his throat.

"Well, if you're sure there's nothing we can do," he said.

"Everything's fine," she said. "How's Karen?"

"She's great, fine," he said.

"I guess we're all just doing swell," Juliet said, exhaling a deep breath to cover her laughter. Her ex-husband always had this effect on her. Exasperation and then amusement. How different he was from a certain man who was scrambling her eggs this morning— and her emotions.

"Did you ever have time to read the letter we sent you, Juliet?" he asked her.

"The one about the investment club? I did look at it briefly, Tony. But I don't—"

"It's really a great idea," he cut in, "you should think about it. It doesn't take much capital and the main company selects the investments so we don't have to make the decision. It's a great way to invest. And I get a little commission on extra investors I bring in," he said proudly.

"You always had ideas," she said, "didn't you, Tony? But I didn't think you had that much money to play with," she said directly. "Or have you quit gambling all together?"

He laughed a little and waved his hand, the one that wore the big diamond pinky ring, bought and sold numerous times.

"I don't gamble anymore, not much anyway, Karen isn't into it, maybe I play the ponies once in a while for old time's sake," he said affably. "Remember how we used to go to the track and you'd wear those big wide-brimmed straw hats? Just like in the movies, Juliet, you were so attractive."

"I wasn't into it either," she said, not amused, "but that didn't stop you, remember? You almost lost our house with your gambling debts."

"Are you going to bring that all up now?" he asked, looking hurt. "That was five years ago."

"I see it as clear as yesterday," she said. "Is it any wonder that I'm not interested in any business schemes of yours?"

"You used to bring me luck," he said, looking at her oddly. "You look thinner, Juliet, are you feeling all right?"

"I'm feeling fine, Tony, especially now that I'm out of debt."

He had the grace to look ashamed.

"I'm sorry about all that, but you know I had a gambling addiction."

"Is it cured?" she asked politely.

"Being married to a nurse is a great equalizer," he said. "She keeps me in line."

And on a budget, I bet, Juliet thought.

"That's great, Tony, I'm glad you got turned around," she said. "But as great as it is to chat, I've got to go. I've got a class tonight."

"Okay, sure, Juliet, I just wanted to stop by." He picked up his keys off the table. "But you won't forget, will you? If you hear of anyone who's looking for a good investment, you'll send them my way, won't you?"

"Absolutely," she assured him.

She worked in the garden, separating some tulip and daffodil bulbs and put in mums and pumpkin plants for the fall. Her granddaughter loved pumpkins. The morning events at the police station had been unsettling; and then finding her ex-husband on her deck had been even more disturbing. It seemed her home was getting to be a meeting place.

She had work to do on the anthology, so she sat down and immersed herself in the poetry of her colleagues and students. Her mind kept wandering; she replayed comparisons between her ex-husband and the man who had scrambled up her garden wall. She had thought she had been in love the first time she married, how could she tell if she was really in love this time? Was she making a mistake, giving away her body, heart, and soul after only knowing Jim a short time?

CHAPTER SEVENTEEN

AT SIX O'CLOCK SHE WAS DRESSING FOR CLASS WHEN THE PHONE rang.

"Hello?" she said softly.

"Miss teacher lady? How goes my Juliet?"

She sighed to herself and smiled. "I'm fine, thank you, how was your day?"

"I was laying concrete and trying to show a lousy plumber where to put a pipe," he said. "Sometimes you gotta do everything yourself if you want things done right."

"You know so much," she said. "You amaze me."

"Thanks, but I gotta lot to learn. Did you go to the police station?"

"I went," she said. "It's done, I've done my civic duty. I'm a law-abiding citizen helping to maintain law and order. And I feel like hell."

"Stay cool," he said. "You did what you had to do. Are you going to school tonight?"

"Of course, I couldn't cancel," she said.

"Need a ride, little girl?"

To the moon, she thought, *with you beside me.*

"No, that's okay, I've got to go to the library first, but thank you for asking."

"No problem," he said, "I've got to check on my favorite teacher, don't I? Gotta make sure she's all right or us axe-murderers won't get any culture or refinement."

"You're hardly an axe-murderer," she said. "Just a student in pursuit of enlightenment."

"I gotta way to go, don't I?" He chuckled softly and it was a caress to her senses.

"A long way," she assured him. "But you're too poetic to be a true deviant."

"Mmmmmm," he said softly, and her heart flipped-flopped hearing the sexy timbre of his voice. "That's good to know that there's hope for me. Oh, and Mrs. West?" he asked.

"Yes, Mr. Sanders?" she asked, equally soft and caressing in her tones.

"Will you go out with me later?" he asked.

"Yes, Mr. Sanders, where would you like to go?"

"I want to show you the moon," he said and hung up.

That's not fair, she thought. *You're not supposed to read my mind.*

She left the house in a dreamy mood. She felt the anxieties of the last week about Charles and her frustration over Jim were gone. She felt good like she finally knew what direction she was going to take. *Take a chance*, she told herself. *You can't lose on love.*

She had a full house tonight at school. Everyone was on time and way in the back, sitting all by himself, was a pirate Romeo, soberly dressed in a dark sports shirt and jeans, but wearing exotic black alligator boots embellished with red stars. She passed back the essays from the week before. She had asked her students to invent another pair of star-crossed lovers and to explain how society could hinder their love. He had written a very lengthy piece about a widow and a silversmith craftsman in eleventh century England who could not marry because she was forty and he was nineteen. This had bothered him. He had said they were star-crossed because society sucked when it came to lovers. If the love affair did not follow the conventions, then it was all wrong, he wrote with vigor. She had made an uncomfortable comment about age differences causing problems down the road and that some ancient wisdoms were not to be laughed at. She had also written a small note about how during the eleventh century with the advent of courtly love, the two could have been tasteful lovers and would have bothered nobody back then.

When she handed him his paper he said, "Thank you, Mrs. West," and looked at her with a face full of love that nearly unhinged her. Then she saw him frowning over her handwritten notes on his paper and she felt a small prickling of apprehension.

"In order to write a good play," she forced herself to focus, "there needs to be a problem to be solved," she said. "In Romeo and Juliet, we found plenty of action and numerous problems. There was the enmity between the Montagues and the Capulets, the wish of Juliet's family for her to marry Paris, the love Romeo and Juliet discover, and the desire to get married and run away. There are also the subplots of Tybalt's death at Romeo's hand and the grave mishap of the apothecary's drug that made Juliet seem dead and caused Romeo to slay himself. There's a lot going on here," she said. "Can anyone venture to tell me what the most important problem of the play might be?"

She looked around the room expectantly. Tonight, there was a hush of shyness. Students looked in the book or at their notes, they looked everywhere but at her.

"Come on, class, I just gave you a half-dozen elements in the plot. Doesn't anyone have an opinion on what is the biggest problem in the play?"

A lone hand raised in the air.

"Yes, Mr. Sanders? Do you have an idea?"

"I have plenty of ideas," he said pleasantly, with an innocent smile, a dangerous smile, "but in answer to your question, I think the biggest problem in the play is trust."

"Can you elaborate on that?" she asked, circling back behind her desk for protection.

"Sure, I can, Mrs. West," he said, still smiling, still innocent. "Now, let me see. I think everyone in this play is just in too much of a hurry."

"You mean, Romeo and Juliet fell in love too fast and should have waited longer before they got married?" she asked, trying to keep her face composed and bland.

"Now wait a moment, Miss teacher, I mean Mrs. West, I didn't say that," he smiled, "I didn't say that at all."

"What are you trying to say then?" she asked, determined to let him make a fool of himself, alone. She wasn't going to join him, but she was afraid she was going to get there with or without his help.

"I mean, they should have trusted in the power of love. They are... here," he opened his book. "*Too rash, too unadvised, too sudden.* And that Friar Laurence guy doesn't help at all. Instead of helping them split out of town, he gets them drugs." An appreciative giggle from one of the girls. "And we know what happens when you put drugs in the hands of teenagers," he added and dropped his voice. "Or sex."

A round of more laughter and agreement.

"You're right," said one student. "Kids are so crazy."

"They should have run away together immediately," said another.

"They needed to be married first," Juliet reminded them. "Before they could escape."

"Yes, but did they have to jump right into bed?" Jim raised the question while more students added their agreement. "Couldn't they have waited?" he asked Juliet.

"I believe when two people fall in love they can be quite impetuous," she said calmly.

"Yes, but were they really in love? Or maybe it was just an infatuation," he pressed on. "Good old-fashioned lust. That happens sometimes, too," he said, with a direct look at her. "Sometimes people fall into bed without truly being in love."

"Then why did they get married?" asked the skinny, serious Hamlet-quoting student in the front of the room.

"Social conventions from the century," Juliet offered. "No sex without marriage in 1400."

"I don't believe that," Jim said. "I believe it was love."

The pretty redhead in the class giggled in appreciation. "Ooh, I like it when a man believes in love," she said. "So many guys just want sex, that's all they think about. And you can't trust them at all when they say they love you."

"See what I mean?" Jim said to the entire room. "How can anyone know what anybody means when it comes to sex and love. I guess it all boils down to trust. Now look here," he riffled through his book, "take this line, when Juliet says to Romeo, *if that thy bent of love be honorable, thy purpose marriage, send me word tomorrow by one, that I'll procure to come to thee,* so she sends the nurse," he explained to the class, "*where and what time thou wilt perform the rite; and all my fortunes at thy foot I'll lay, and follow thee my lord throughout the world.* See?" he asked everybody. "One kiss and she's ready to marry him and follow him around the world. Gee, if I could only find a woman like that these days. I would be the happiest of men."

"I'm sure there are plenty of women who believe in marriage and fidelity," Juliet said, trying to seize back control of the discussion. "As did Juliet. But the feud between the Montagues and the Capulets was so strong that Romeo and Juliet were afraid to run away. And then the tragedy when Romeo kills Juliet's cousin, I'm afraid that's when fate steps in and begins to throw them a curve at every turn. Since Romeo was banished from Verona, it would be hard for Juliet to follow him. She was heavily watched and protected. After all, it was the fifteenth century,"

Juliet said, with a smile. "So, trust was hindered by social conventions."

"She should have told her old man that she had married Romeo and couldn't stand Paris," Jim said. "She should have trusted in the power of love."

"She was afraid," Juliet said, starting to get flustered. "Her father might have sent her to a nunnery or could have banished her for years. Parents had all the control."

"Then Romeo could have gotten his band of merry men and rescued her," Jim said, crossing his arms in front of his taut body. "If he had really loved her, he would have found a way to rescue her."

"He wasn't Robin Hood," said Juliet, getting upset. "He was Romeo. He was a dreamer and a poet," Juliet said. "I'm not sure he would have known how to rescue her."

"I know all about poets," he said, taking a direct slam at her. "He should have stayed with his old girlfriend, the babe the family approved of," he said in disgust. "He shouldn't be a wimp if he's in love."

"Not all men feel like you," she said, "some men are more cautious or fearful or whatever you want to call it."

"I call it trust," he said smugly. "They haven't trusted in the power of their love. The love gives them strength and wisdom to do the right thing."

"It does?" she asked softly. The whole room was quietly watching them. Tension filled the air.

"Yeah, immeasurable power, the strength of titans," he said, looking at her. "But some men don't believe that. Look at Romeo, he finds Juliet asleep and thinks she's dead. Why couldn't he have waited for a doctor or that darned Friar who screwed everything up? No, he has to take poison and croak himself. It's ridiculous," he said scornfully.

"She was in the family vault. Everyone thought she was dead,"

Juliet said. "You would need the trust and the wisdom of the universe to believe otherwise."

Jim stood up and looked at her. "I would have believed. I would have trusted in the power of love and beauty. I wouldn't have let her out of my sight for one minute if I had truly loved her, I don't care how old I was; fifteen or forty-five. Or how old she was; fifteen or fifty-five," he said pointedly. Juliet felt her cheeks starting to flush. He wasn't going to humiliate her in front of her class, was he?

"That's what I would have done. Dragged her right off to be married and then gotten the hell out of town," he said, tossing the book down on his desk.

"Not everyone has as much strength as you do," Juliet said cautiously.

"No, and not everyone can trust," he harked back to his old theme. "If I had known that taking literature in college was going to break my heart and make me hate poetry I would never have signed up," he said with a bitter look at her. "I thought, I trusted that this would be good for me," he picked up the pink Penguin edition of Romeo and Juliet and looked at it one last time. "I was wrong, wasn't I?"

"Mr. Sanders," she said, taking a deep breath. "I'm sure that Shakespeare didn't want to upset you."

He looked straight at her as he walked to the door. He dropped the book on an empty desk.

"Maybe he doesn't, but lady, you sure do," he said, and walked out of the classroom and out of her life.

CHAPTER EIGHTEEN

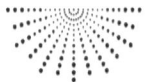

HER CLASS HANDLED THE WALK OUT VERY WELL. AFTER A MOMENT of shock, everyone exhaled as one and began to talk. Juliet picked up her water bottle off her desk and took a deep swallow. She had forgotten all about her comments on his essay. How sensitive he was, how little she knew about him.

"Hey, class, this is just like the 60's, right?" she asked with an attempt at levity. "Abbie Hoffman, Woodstock and the Chicago Democratic Convention, which by the way, took place not too far from here," she said. "Most of you are too young to remember these events, but Mr. Sanders seems to be good at protests and walk-outs."

"Ooh, he was really mad at you," another girl said. "He must have a thing for you, to walk out like that."

"I'm sure that's not it," Juliet lied. "He's probably just having a mid-life crisis." More laughter and the moment of embarrassment had passed. She took the opportunity to work in Jim's moment of temper with the play. "Maybe Juliet's father and mother were having a marital crisis and took it out on their daughter," she suggested. "They were unhappy in their own marriage and were trying to marry her off, couldn't that be so?"

Heads nodded in agreement and thought. "If her mother wasn't happy with her father, then she couldn't have stood it, that Juliet was so pretty and admired and loved. She would have liked to have seen her married off to man she didn't love, which probably mirrored her own past," Juliet explained.

"How do you explain that guy walking out because of a little Shakespeare?" asked another young man. "He seemed pretty intense to me. I hope he's not going to come back and waste us. I heard what nearly happened to you the other night, Mrs. West."

By the time the smoke cleared after the whole room learned about her abduction at gunpoint by a former student and the redhead insisted that Jim *was* in love with Mrs. West to her intense discomfort, the class was over.

"It's time," she said. "Nine o'clock. We didn't cover much tonight," she said apologetically. "We'll pick it up again on Thursday. Please read the rest of the play by then."

"I think we covered plenty," the redhead said, with eyes that sparkled with interest. "And I think most of it was about you, Mrs. West."

She had never wanted to be notorious. Famous, yes. A famous poet, a great mother, a person who did something for society. But she had never expected to be a notorious lady who was abducted by a former student and who was put in the spotlight by a former student who was in love with her. *Former student*, she realized how her thoughts were going. Would he ever come back to her class?

She swiftly packed up and hurried out of the building. Her daughter was due home in a couple of days and this was a great consolation to her frazzled nerves and tormented soul. Just to feel the arms of her granddaughter around her neck would soothe her. *I've made such a mistake, with Jim. I've handled him all wrong. He's got the soul of the poet and I'm the ditchdigger,* she thought. Who would have guessed?

In the parking lot, she ran into a colleague, bumping bookbags in the dim light.

"Sorry, Miss, I mean, Juliet," Dr. Whiteside said in astonishment. "My God, in this light, you look eighteen."

"It's very dark out here. But thank you for the compliment," she said with a laugh.

He looked at her closely. "No, my dear, it's not the light. It's you. You're looking positively luminous and breathtakingly young. Are you taking some new kind of vitamin?"

She laughed in happiness. "Yes, I am," she told him, "it's a new vitamin. And it's wonderful."

"Call my wife," he shouted after her. "Give her the name of it, will you?"

"Okay, I will," she laughed over her shoulder. "I definitely will."

How can I? she asked herself, pinching her arm one last time. *The name of this vitamin, this elixir of youth, is love.*

She threw her bags in the car and ran across the campus to the drama department. There she found one of her oldest and best college friends, sewing a costume amid frantic rehearsal noises of a Greek play.

"Hi, Katy," Juliet said. "What is it tonight? Euripides?"

"No," the woman said, holding up a pair of trousers. "I rip-a 'dese."

"Ouch," Juliet said, laughing. "So much for culture."

"Hey, this isn't Broadway, as much as I love this school and these kids," her friend said. "What can I do for you, Lady Juliet?"

Juliet's eyes widened at the name. "It must show," she said. "Please, can you lend me a costume, Katy dear?"

Her friend's eyes sparkled. "This sounds very interesting, my love. Would you care to explain it to me?"

Juliet did and she was rewarded with a costume *too rich for use and for earth too dear.* The ornate dress and cap were now draped over her tall, voluptuous body; the burgundy velvet trimmed with gold braid hugged her ample bosom and flared over her hips. The train of her gown was embroidered with doves and roses. The cap was gold and black satin and fastened under her chin with a woven silk strap.

She saw the security guard's startled but amused eyes and she tried to look calm and collected as she drove away. *What am I doing? Is this madness? I hope he's home,* she thought nervously. *And alone.*

She followed the familiar streets to an unfamiliar neighborhood across town. It was a quiet neighborhood, with large well-kept lawns and basketball hoops in the driveways. She found his street and slowly drove down it, hoping the neighbors wouldn't think a middle-aged woman dressed like an Italian countess from the 1400's too weird a sight and call the cops on her. She couldn't find the right address and realized she had missed his house by a block. Juliet pulled over and drummed her fingers on the steering wheel.

What was she doing? What if he laughed at her, or even worse, refused to answer the door? She decided that she could deal with rejection, but not with apathy. She drove ruthlessly on.

Finally, she found the right house. She drove by and saw the lights were on. She hoped his sons weren't having a party and think she was a psycho guest, *but faint heart never won fair gentleman*, she paraphrased in her head. Especially one with boots, a tattoo and an earring.

She pulled around the corner and into the alley. Here, she felt safe and felt sure she could pull off the fantasy. She parked her car behind his garage, got out carefully, and looked up into the darkness at his deck. It was a lovely, huge cedar deck, much grander and more costly than hers and she could see the bright light of a wide-screened TV and hear the cheers of a baseball game from where she stood. The deck was deserted although she smelled the strong aroma of a cigar and brewing coffee. Also, a tinge of hot pizza filled the air. She immediately got hungry, thirsty and wanted to use the bathroom. *I'm nervous,* she thought. What if somebody comes out to dump the garbage? *Think fast,* Juliet.

In her nervous hand, she held the pink book, his discarded copy of the play. She held it against her chest and tried to work up her nerve. She took a handful of pebbles from the garden and threw them up over the side of the deck. *Take that,* she thought. *I'll stumble on your counsel.*

She heard a male voice and then another. From above, a bright light shone down on her head, blinding her eyes.

"What the?" then a delighted laugh. Then another.

"Dad, oh Dad," called a familiar voice. The younger version of her lover.

"Da-ad," called the second voice. "Come out here, we want you to see something."

"Hi, Mrs. West," Randy called down. "You look great. Are you taking my dad to a costume party or something?"

"Not quite, I'm not expected and I feel like a fool. Is your dad available? Will he talk to me?" she asked, smoothing down her velvet skirt with nervous fingers.

"He's home," said the other twin. "And he's available. Hi, I'm Mike. I've heard a lot about you, Mrs. West."

"Hi, nice to meet you, I've heard a lot about you, too," she said, hoping that the whole clan wasn't going to show up to inspect her. "What's your father doing?"

"Getting drunk and smoking cigars and talking about moving to Alaska," said Mike. "Whenever he has a problem, he talks about moving."

"But when it's a real big problem he wants to sell everything and move to Alaska," Randy said. "Congratulations, Mrs. West, 'cause he's got the maps out."

She looked at the two young handsome men, shorter but very virile carbon copies of their father. She smiled, feeling her foolishness fading away. They looked like they liked her and were going to be her allies.

"I wonder if you wouldn't mind calling him out here for a minute," she said. "I'd like to talk to him."

"Come on up," Randy said with enthusiasm. "You don't have to stand outside, we'd love to have you come in."

His brother swatted his arm. "I don't think that's the point, Randy," Mike said. "I'm guessing that Mrs. West has a little more in mind than just coming up," he said, looking at her fancy costume.

"Oh, I get it, you want to say some poetry or something like out of a movie," Randy said. "Gosh, Dad's lucky. But he's in such a foul mood, I hope he likes your costume."

Mike smiled. "No worries, I know he will. I'll go get him."

She was left alone in the alley with her thoughts. She heard a barrage of male voices and then she heard footsteps on the deck. She saw a golden pirate head leaning over the side, peering down at her and she took a chance.

"*But soft, what light through yonder window breaks?*" she said sweetly. "*It is the east and James is the sun.*"

"What the—why, could it be my Miss teacher lady, coming to call, real social like on a Tuesday evening?" he drawled down at her. "Why I can't believe my whiskey-soaked eyes."

"You shouldn't drink so much," she said reprovingly, "it's bad for your health."

"Lady, you are bad for my health," he said, and looked down at her, his eyes widening in surprise and admiration. "Nice duds."

"*Tis but thy name that is my enemy,*" she plunged on. "*What's in a name? That which we call a rose by any other name would smell as sweet. So James would, were he not James called, retain that dear perfection which he owes without that title.*" She took the pink book out of her pocket and held it up for him to see. "*Jim darling, doff thy name, and for thy name, which is no part of thee, take all myself.*"

She tossed the book up to him. "Here, catch," she said. "You left this in school."

"Are you the visiting bookmobile?" he asked, with a look that could melt a lesser mortal.

"Something like that," she said.

"Is the bookmobile open for customers?" he said with a wicked look.

"Very open," she said sincerely.

He took the book and raised it to his face. He inhaled deeply. "Ah, the smell of culture, refinement and you, Juliet. God, I was mad at you tonight."

"I wrote those comments on your paper when I didn't know you so well," she said.

"We had made love," he said.

"I know, I know, but I was mixed up and feeling vulnerable. I had never dated a playboy, you see—"

"A playboy?" he hooted with laughter. "Lady, you don't know me at all. I'm not a playboy, I'm a old, tired Marine, trying to make a living, raise my kids and get over a broken heart. You were—are—a breath of fresh life to me. Newness and purity and hope," he said, gazing down at her. What she saw in his eyes took *her* breath away. "I know I'm talking crazy, because I've been drinking and smoking cigars and cigar smoke makes me dizzy but believe me," he opened the book and read, *"I'll prove more true than those that have more cunning to be strange. I should have been more strange, I must confess,* but when I met you, honey," here he lapsed into the now, *"I felt my true love's passion. Therefore pardon me,* for being such a jealous jerk, *and not impute this yielding to light love, which the dark night hath so discovered."*

"Your point?" she asked him, laughing in delight.

"My point?" he repeated softly. "Lady, I'm in love with you."

"I know," she said in a whisper. "I know that now."

"And I keep asking you to marry me and I keep getting hit in the chin," he said, shaking his golden head in regret.

"I'm sorry. I'm not used to proposals of marriage from pirate Romeos. I've been very difficult, haven't I?"

"Difficult? You've been one royal pain in the—"

"Do not swear," she cut in, *"or, if thou wilt, swear by thy gracious self... and I'll believe thee."*

"Your point?" he asked her, hand on hip, cigar burning in the dark.

"I love you, James, and I do want to marry you," she said, feeling humbled by her admission.

"You what?" he half-shouted, eyes wide open with pleasure.

"I will marry you, if you still want me to, I mean if you think you do—"

"Oh, Lady Juliet, I can't believe that you really love me!" he flew down the stairs and in a second was by her side. He grabbed her and kissed her passionately.

"I do love you, I've been afraid to admit it, everything happened so quickly," she murmured into his searching mouth. "Gee, that cigar smoke stinks," she gasped.

"I know, I'm sorry, I'll take a shower real soon," he moaned, as he covered her with kisses. "I want to hold you all night in my arms."

"Where?" she asked with a smile.

"Good point," he conceded, kissing her neck and face until she was breathless. "I can send my sons to a hotel, or over to a friend," he offered.

"No, I don't want to put them out of their home," she said. "Come over and stay with me, tonight."

"You sure?" he asked her huskily. "Because if I come over there's no turning back."

She knew that to be true. He had made an effort to romance her and to protect her and she could not turn down his offer of love again. His pride couldn't take it and she wouldn't expect him to. He was so strong and she would get used to his strength.

He nuzzled her ear and caressed her back.

"We're going to fight all the time," she said.

"I know it," he whispered into her ear. "I like a good argument with a beautiful woman. It makes the making up after all the sweeter."

"Why did you come to college anyway," she said in wonder. "You seem to have all the poetry and refinement you could ever want. Classes don't teach it to you. It's something innate, something that blossoms," she said, kissing his mouth tenderly.

"This bud of love really bloomed, didn't it?" he asked huskily. "And much better than I thought."

From above, the voices of his sons.

"What's going on, Dad? Do you need help?"

"I can handle this myself," Jim called up to them. "But boys, you'll have to watch the castle alone tonight, I've got to go scramble up a balcony across town."

"What?" Randy asked. "What balcony?"

Juliet and Jim walked arm in arm to her car.

"I'll tell you tomorrow," Jim said to them. He put his arm around her tenderly; she melted into his embrace.

"I never thought I'd fall in love teaching Shakespeare," she said, glowing with the anticipation of the night ahead of them.

PLEASE REVIEW

We hope you enjoyed *Hot for Teacher - Shakespeare Made Us Fall in Love* by Felicia Carparelli. If you did, we would ask that you please rate and review this title. Every review helps our authors.

Rate and Review: Hot for Teacher - Shakespeare Made Us Fall in Love

MEET THE AUTHOR

Felicia Carparelli is a public-school teacher and writer in Chicago. She has been published in FlexxMag, The Rhubris, Coping with Cancer, Cure Today, Chicken Soup, the New York Times and the Chicago Sun-Times. Gotham Writer's workshops have helped shape her writing.

She belongs to the Romance Writers of America, Chicago Writers Association, and the Wacker Drive Writers Group.

She loves Jane Austen. She lives on the river with her Chin-Pin, Presley two parakeets and pictures of her family everywhere.

She enjoys writing books in different genres—romances, mysteries and YA novels.

PUBLISHER ACKNOWLEDGEMENTS

The team at 5 Prince Publishing would like to give special thanks to the following people for helping make Hot for Teacher - Shakespeare Made Us Fall in Love the best that it can be:

Bernadette Soehner, Cate Byers, Marianne Nowicki, Sophie Jefferson, Cayla Rusielewicz, and Lindsey Haggerty. We would also like to thank our Brand Ambassadors, touring companies, bloggers, and influencers that help to promote the work of Felicia Carparelli.